SONS OF THE SWORDMAKER

## BY MAURICE WALSH

# SONS OF
# THE SWORDMAKER

By
MAURICE WALSH

W. & R. CHAMBERS, LTD.
38 SOHO SQUARE, LONDON, W.1
AND EDINBURGH

**7/6 Edition**

*Published September 1938*
*Reprinted October 1938*

**3/6 Edition**

*Published September 1939*

Printed in Ireland at The Talbot Press, Dublin.

DEDICATED
TO MY SONS
AND I AM NO SWORDMAKER

# CONTENTS

# FOREWORD.

LET the chronology be set down that all men may dispute it.

At that time Joseph, in his middle years, was still unmarried and no more than a fair-to-middling journeyman carpenter in the hillfoot towns about Jerusalem. Great Caesar had been daggered these score of years; and Octavian, after the victory of Actium, was become Augustus but not yet Pontifex Maximus.

At that time Spain had been divided into three Roman provinces; the Gauls had been conquered for good and evil and had lain for a generation, under a sane and desolating peace; the Germans, under Arminius, were still free; the South Britons were paying a small tribute to Rome; the Wall of Hadrian across North Britain, that sullen final outpost of the Empire, would not be built for yet a full hundred years; and the Scots and Picts of Erin and Alba had not yet faced a Roman legion and broken it.

At that time Conmac the White Fox was King of North Britain; Ingcel One-Eye, his son, was

Prince of Cumbria ; Gabur the Red was Chief of Ormlyth ; Tulchinne of the Rapine was Regent of the Picts of Strathclyde. Conchobar was King of Ulster, but Cuchulain was dead, and dead was golden Deirdre on the breast of Naoise ; Maeve the Proud was Queen of Connacht, tamed Fergus under her hand ; and, finally, Conaire the Great was High King of Erin at Royal Tara. Of Conaire more shall be heard.

Let the chronicle begin now.

# PART I.

## FACE OF STONE.

# SONS OF THE SWORDMAKER.

## CHAPTER I.

### *The Swordmaker.*

In their own time and in their own gathering way the stories of the blood fights of Urnaul, and of his failure to possess the red woman, Alor, came home to Long Baravais beyond the mountains that hedge in the vast high plain of The Ser. There in that pleasant hamlet, where the squat friendly houses are strung out along the slope below the pines and above green levels of Rem, lived Urnaul's father and the four brothers of Urnaul. This chronicle tells all there is to be told, or a little, of these four brothers.

Their father, Orugh, old only in years, ruddy, grizzled, padded in sound flesh, wide as a door, was an easy-going man who prided himself on a doubtful virtue he did not possess : steadfastness. His sons knew that he had many virtues, but that he was not steadfast. They would agree that he was a trace obstinate on occasion, yet easily relenting, forgetting anger with the cooling of his blood and his desperately sworn enmities after a night's sleep ; and they would point out that the reason he had most of his own way was because his own way was a good way, and it pleased them to let him have it. He disputed with them as his equals—almost—was happy with his own logic, and was careful to leave an impression that there was something to be said on their side, too, poor lads. By trade he was a swordmaker, and a notable one.

Delgaun was the oldest brother. He was a grave, taciturn, dark man who held reason as the only god. In his youth, like all the wandering men of Baravais, he had taken to the road, but he had worn no sword, and no one had heard one word of him—by name—for ten years. Then he had come home, and, though he was not old, he had put youth behind him for all time. He moored himself in his own haven of the mind, took thought before giving tongue, and held steadfastly by a peace that hid some old unquiet at its core. Sometimes, not often, he would say a word or two of places he had seen—Rome of the Commonwealth, Spain of the soldiers, the strange islands beyond the grey Northern Sea—but no single word could be got from him of the things he had done, or had not done. Such was Delgaun.

Cond came next to Delgaun and was his half-brother. He was a giant of a man and handsome, with crisp brown curls, blue eyes, white teeth, and the jaw of a fighter. He was a great lover and a merry laugher, but, besides these, he was held to be the best swordsman in Long Baravais now that Urnaul was blood-letting in The Ser to ensure that no man but Urnaul be the father of red Alor's son.

Flann was the third brother, and he was full-brother to Cond. He was lean, long-jawed, horse-headed, with a corrosive tongue, a sour rind, and a kind core. His brothers bore with the corrosive tongue, for they made full use of the kind core. Anything they wanted done, and had not time or will to do, they put upon Flann, and Flann, having spoken his mind mordantly, invariably did it.

Maur was the youngest son of Orugh. He was full-brother to Delgaun and Urnaul, and half-brother to Cond and Flann. A stripling of twenty, with darkly-fair waving hair, a live mouth, and eyes like a deer's; his skin was olive-brown and as delicately smooth as a girl's, and a girl like him would have lovers in plenty. He was the apple of his father's eye, and to Delgaun he was calf to cow, perhaps, because he was not unlike that long-dead Delgaun who had left youth behind him in some bitter corner of the world.

Young Maur was the talker of the family. He had a theory about most things, and would have a theory about everything if he knew that far. He others were giving tongue—which he made sure was not too often—that he paced steadily on the packed clay.

"Alor is older than all the tales, and all the great tales have been about her," he repeated, and looked up at Delgaun.

It was the derisive Flann that took him up.

"Three times wrong in one breath—you will never do better, young Maur."

"I said only one thing," protested Maur.

"And you were wrong three times. Whatever else she is, Alor is not old. There was never a great tale of Alor or any other woman, but, good or bad, there were tales of this woman and that before Alor was born. Three times, milk-tooth!"

"Sourface!" said Maur witheringly.

"The thing that Maur says," said the sober Delgaun, "is that Alor is one of a long line."

"She is," cried Maur. "She is the ever-living One-without-mercy. No man knows where her glamour sits to grasp it, and Urnaul is only her sword-hand. She is one of the golden women that caused wars, and the dark ones that sapped the strength of men."

"She is a red woman, they say," put in Orugh.

"Even so. A red woman that stays in a man's mind! That is what a man, who had seen her, told me yesterday, and that is all that stayed in his mind to tell me."

"Speaking of tales," said Cond, "when I was young——"

"When did you grow old, codger?" Flann wanted to know.

"When I was young," repeated Cond firmly, "there was that tale of a woman in Far Mussoul who was so beautiful and so wicked that her judges, to condemn her, had to be blindfolded."

"You would like to judge that woman, but not blindfolded," hinted Flann.

"I mind that woman well," said Orugh. "She was the one that the terrible Stone-Face did all the killing for. And when the people killed her, Stone-Face disappeared as if under the ground, and no one has seen or heard of him to this day."

"Delgaun was out and about the world that time," suggested Flann slyly.

Delgaun moved his head slowly in assent.

"Did you see that wicked one, Delgaun? Maybe you loved her?"

"She was made that way," said Delgaun, in his slow, heavy way, "but she was not wicked."

"Oh!" There was surprise in Flann's tone. "A wonder you did not try a clout at Stone-Face?"

"That is no wonder," said Delgaun soberly.

"No wonder at all," agreed his father. "Delgaun had no sword."

"They say that Stone-Face used borrow a sword and kill with the first blow," hinted Flann.

"You are not saying that Delgaun was Stone-Face? That is foolish, even for you. Delgaun was never a swordsman"; and Orugh added regretfully, "though he has the wrist and the thigh-bone."

"You were talking of Urnaul and the woman Alor, small brother?" Delgaun put to Maur.

"Let him talk away," cried Orugh. "What I say is that Urnaul will have his way with her. Look at the virtues to him! Steadfast, deep as a well, not readily touched, not to be turned aside, constant——"

"Obstinate!" added Flann.

"All his virtues and all his faults! You have put your finger on them, my father," said Maur of the theories. "He will never have his way with the woman that is Alor."

"What do you know of the woman that is Alor, young one?" derided Flann.

"There is a picture of her in my mind's eye. I know her to the marrow of her bones. She has red hair and she stays in a man's mind. Brief enough, but enough. She draws men and men draw her—one pull goes with the other always. But hidden in her is a cold virgin that has some secret high ideal of her own. Time and again she

thinks her ideal alive in a hero here and there, a
man like Urnaul—a man like Cond here——''

"What about yourself?" Cond wanted to
know.

Maur smiled and flushed. "It is true that I am
thinking of myself too," he said frankly. "But
let that be. The point I make is that the cold virgin
takes fright when the hero becomes the male——"

"What else would a hero become?" Flann
scoffed.

"Nothing in his power, and there is the heart
of the trouble. She means no harm, but the harm
is done despite her; she is no vampire, but she
drains the joy of living out of a man; she has no
guile, but she might as well be wiled like the
serpent. That is Alor! And here is our Urnaul!
Urnaul the Steadfast, not to be turned aside, as
my father says! Not able to turn aside, I say!
He moves in his own groove, and is sure, as Death
is sure, that Alor, who once seemed to love him,
must always love him. The flame in him must
flame in her, consume her, as it consumes him,
unquenchably, delight her and delight him till time
be done. Let all men beware! Alor is Urnaul's
woman. Who dare question it? Draw and die
then! And that is Urnaul."

"That indeed is Urnaul," agreed Delgaun
weightily.

" The whole bloody business is clear then, and I need say no more," cried Maur triumphantly.

" You said a good deal, long-talker," said Flann.

" What I still say," persisted Orugh obstinately, " is that Urnaul will have his way with that woman—or any woman. He is the best man of his hands between here and wherever he is."

" But woman is not an affair of hands, old fellow," objected Flann.

" Speaking of hands," said Cond, jealous for his own, " Urnaul has good ones, but not as good as his father thinks."

" He is the best swordsman I ever made a sword for," insisted Orugh.

" Do not boast him, Orugh," warned Flann. " The last we heard of him he was in The Ser, and I mind you made a sword for a man in that place."

" That was Fergus of Running Water," said Cond quickly, and frowned. " He is one of the great ones for all his lack of thew. I saw him at a practice-bout once. A rod of iron, and light as a blown leaf, no one could hold his blade engaged."

" Then there is only one way to beat him," declared Maur.

" You have the trick, little brother ? " Cond grinned.

" I will give it to you, Cond. Hold his blade

engaged till you are ready to strike the killing blow."

Cond laughed merrily. " I have it now. Every man that tried Fergus tried that, and they are all dead or handless."

" It is the only way, nevertheless," Delgaun backed up Maur.

" Hear the skilled man talk ! " derided Flann. " You would think that Stone-Face had come out of his hole to kill with his one blow."

" That man is dead," said Delgaun soberly.

" How do you know ? "

" I stood on his grave."

" Oh ! " Again Flann was surprised. " That is the first I heard of it."

" It will be the last you will hear of it also," said Delgaun, and pointed a long arm down the slope towards the green levels of Rem. " Look ! Here is Ager the Blender homing from Rem Hove ! "

# CHAPTER II.

## *The Sword Comes Home.*

AGER THE BLENDER, expert in cordials, rode the
top of the high green bank of Rem River nearly
half a mile distant.   So rare was the evening air
that the legs of the pony he bestrode could be seen
like black knitting-needles busy against the levels
of the marsh.   The hunched rider sat far back on
the crupper, and his feet wagged below the pony's
belly.   Two full panniers balanced before him.

It was an evening of late fall, and after a day of
sun and haze the air had become crystal-clear and
with a pleasant hint of shrewdness to it.   The
usually soft lines of Rem Marsh were now drawn
surely, and the high embankment of Rem River
curved across its breast like a ribbon.   At the very
limit of distance the mountains that upheld the
plateau of The Ser had taken on substance, and
peak rose behind purple peak etched as with a point
of silver.   Dead in the west the ball of the sun hung
poised above the gold bar of the sea, and the long,
grotesque, dark shadow of Ager and his pony

moved smoothly across the orange-lit green of the marsh grasses. The wild duck were beginning to flight inland, and, ever and again, the hiss of their short hurrying wings went overhead. But for that sound and the faint thin song of the evening midgets there was a stillness that filled the bowl of the sky. And in that stillness Orugh and his four sons watched Ager homing it from Rem Hove.

Maur was first to break the silence. He is not at his singing this evening. Too much Rem spirits ! ''

'' He would sing full to the thrapple and sing better than you,'' Flann told him.

'' You would say that, right or wrong, horse-face,'' Maur retorted.

Ager turned off the embankment to the pony track that, fifty paces below, wound the length of the township.

'' Give him a hail, Orugh,'' urged Cond.

'' No. He might not like us to see, and he carrying too much of his own load inside him.''

But when Ager came to the side-track leading up to the house he turned in without pausing, as if he had already decided to pay a visit.

'' The old hero ! '' commented Orugh. '' He wants us to taste his new spirits.''

'' He might have news or a fresh tale,'' said Maur a trifle sourly. This Ager of the hollow cheeks and domed brow was reputed the best story-teller in Long Baravais, and Maur knew that he was not.

It was then that Orugh had his twinge of foreboding, and it made him lift his voice to the approaching rider.

" Welcome, fine man ! What do you bring ? "

Ager raised a hand in reply. " A sword, my sorrow," he muttered to himself, and drew rein at the bar of the sun-porch.

" You have it with you," observed Cond.

He meant the two small casks balanced in the panniers, but Ager took him up differently.

" I have it with me," he said seriously. " How did the news come to ye ? "

He placed his hand on the chased hilt of a sword that hung, long and lean, from a loop over his shoulder. The four sons looked at the sword and looked at their father, and their father, before he spoke, drew in a long breath through open mouth.

" We have no news," he said. " Is it Urnaul ? "

" Urnaul it is. This is the sword you made for him. He is dead, Orugh."

" I know he is dead, Ager. Who killed him ? "

" Fergus of Running Water in The Ser."

" In fair fight ? "

" Fair, as I heard it."

" We were talking of Fergus," said Orugh.

" Fergus the killer was the one man I was afraid

of always," confessed Cond frankly. "I will not be afraid of him any more."

Old Orugh gathered up his thoughts. "Come off your horse, Ager, and tell us what you know."

"I will, friend."

He pivoted to the ground, slung the reins over the rail, and lifted himself stiffly to the porch. There he unslung the sheathed sword and laid it across Orugh's knees; and Orugh laid his hand softly on the cross of the hilt.

"It is the sword I made for him," he said quietly.

Flann drew forward the bench, and Ager, sighing deeply, sat down amongst them.

"It is not pleasant to be the bringer of bad news," he said, "but someone had to bring it. The word came to Rem Hove this morning."

The five kin of dead Urnaul waited silently, and each behaved in his own way. Orugh sat looking down at his hands crossed on the cross of the sword; Delgaun, sitting on the edge of the stoop, had drawn his heels up and looked out across the marsh over his clasped knees, still as a rock, strangely aloof, as if he had drawn himself deep down and away from all this mad business of blood and love; Cond's strong teeth were clenched so that the muscles of his jaw stood out; Flann's nose twitched, and the sardonic line deepened at mouth corner; and Maur, sitting close to Delgaun,

27

watched the story-teller with frowning eyes that held a trace of jealousy.

"A trireme for Rome put in at Rem Hove with the morning tide," Ager began in his easy story-teller's way. "She was on her half-yearly passage from Cahen of The Ser with a cargo of wine, and her master landed at the point to bargain for a butt of our graded spirits—and a sound judge he was. I was there when he landed—six or seven of us kicking our heels amongst the puncheons. 'Is that Long Baravais yonder under the pine hills?' That is how he began. 'Well you know it, Colle,' said I, 'and you calling at Rem Hove twice a season these ten years! Yes, that is Long Baravais, and I live there.' 'So you do, Ager,' he said, 'and maybe you knew a tall, swart hero named Urnaul?' 'I knew him and I know him,' I told him. 'The best swordsman from the hills to the sea, and the son of my friend, Orugh, the swordmaker.' 'You are the man I am looking for,' said he then, 'and thank you for saving me a journey and an unlikeable task at the end of it. It could be that Urnaul was the best swordsman about here, but he was not the best in The Ser. Fergus of Running Water killed him in a fight three weeks ago come to-morrow morning.' And that is how I heard it, Orugh."

Orugh glanced at him. "He told you about the fight?"

"He did, and I would not believe it at first. But the shipmaster, sitting there on one of my own kegs, was sure of it. 'I saw the fight and the finish,' said he, 'and here is Urnaul's sword that Fergus put in my hands to bring back to Urnaul's father—and to his brothers.'"

"It is what a fighting man would do," said Cond in his teeth. "Go on, Ager!"

"Colle is a man of The Ser himself, and, while his boat was taking in cargo, he went inland to a place called Alder Hollow on the far side to see his brother. The woman, Alor, that we hear so much about, was there. She was living in Alder Hollow—she had been living there a month or more in a small hut by herself. No! Urnaul was not with her when Colle arrived, but he came down over the brink of the plain that very evening. Whether she was pleased or not pleased the shipmaster did not know, but, maybe, she was, for Urnaul was in the best of humour. He gave some of the youths a lesson-bout in the ring, and only laughed when a venturesome one kept hovering about the red-haired she-devil. Indeed and indeed, all might have gone well that time if someone had not sent word down to Running Water, which is only a mile or so below in the same valley——"

"Someone would do just that, and be very

careful of his own skin," said Flann, angrily bitter.

" That is true. Anyhow, Fergus the killer came strolling up in the morning, and with Urnaul and Fergus and the woman in one place the swords soon began to stir in their sheaths."

" Was it the woman started the trouble between them ? " Maur asked quickly.

" The very question I put to Colle, and he was not sure. ' Maybe she was and maybe she was not,' he said. ' Fergus, the world knows, needs small excuse to draw blade, and the blade was soon taking the sun.' Colle saw it all, and he says that he heard most of what was said."

Ager, like a good story-teller, paused to visualise the scene in his own mind. " According to the shipmaster, Fergus came up to Urnaul like a fighting cock, head out and knees stiff-strutting in that way he has. ' I am Fergus of Running Water,' he says. ' I hear you are Urnaul of Rem and a fighting man.' ' That is my name,' said Urnaul, ' and I fight for cause given.' Fergus laughed—he laughs easily, but it is not good laughter—and said he, ' That is your way. Myself I fight, cause or no cause, but what cause would make you fight ? ' And he looked at Alor. She was standing by, and heard what was said. She came close to them, looking from one to the other. ' Do not make me a cause,' said she. ' Ye two will fight.' No, it was not an order. It was saying a thing she knew, and she was sad saying it. Colle could not get her out of his head. She came between them and spoke to Urnaul. ' Do not fight, Urnaul.' And Urnaul said—I can hear the slow weight of his voice—' I will not fight, Alor, unless cause is given, or I am challenged.' And again Fergus laughed. ' I compel no man to fight me,' he said, ' but, all the same, I would like a small bout with the great Urnaul.' And Urnaul cried aloud, ' That is a challenge.' Alor laughed, bitter and angry. ' Let it be so,' she said. ' Fight if ye like and kill if ye like—ye are no men of mine.' And she turned and left them.''

Delgaun, who did not seem to be listening, groaned deeply.

'' The thing started as easy as that. In no time at all they were facing each other in the ring before all the people. It was a good fight as the sailor told it, but, being of The Ser, he had a side for Fergus. Myself, I will never believe that there was a better swordsman than Urnaul south of the Four Seas—not even you, Cond, not even the terrible Stone-Face that was in Far Mussoul.''

'' Fergus killed him, I would remind you,'' said Flann.

'' He did. It was a skilly bout, without targes, growing slowly to deadliness and still skilly. That is Fergus's way. He is a slow killer, and Urnaul took many wounds. And there was blood on Fergus too." He threw his hands wide in a gesture of finality. "But why should I hurt you? Urnaul fell at last, and died that night in Alor's hut."

"He was taken to her hut?" came the heavy voice of Delgaun.

"She saw him taken and held his head on her lap, and she wept over him when he died. 'If she wept over me,' said the shipmaster, 'I would wake again.' But Urnaul did not wake."

"Is she still in that place, Alder Hollow?" Maur asked.

"I could not tell you, but she was there during the four days Colle stayed—and he did not want to leave. And Fergus, who loves swording better than any woman, was wondering when the next hardy man would be lured that way."

"The hardy man will come that way," said Maur boldly, "and Fergus will know it."

Delgaun shook his heavy head, and Orugh stirred in his chair.

"Fergus sent back the sword?" Cond had that on his mind.

"With Colle, as I told you."

"It is what a fighting man would do. Is there no more, Ager?"

"One thing only——"

Ager hesitated. His eyes rested on Delgaun

who was the oldest brother and full-brother to dead Urnaul. But Delgaun sat still, aloof as an idol, shoulders hunched over his knees, and his gaze out over the marshes of Rem, turning wan and desolate in the desolate afterlight. Then Ager's eyes moved past Maur and Flann, and stopped on Cond's.

"Fergus sent a message with the sword, Ager?" prompted Cond, and clenched his teeth.

"He did, Cond. This is it : 'Tell Orugh and his sons that Fergus can be found if one of them would like to try what Urnaul tried.' That is all."

"It is the message of a fighting man," said Cond.

Ager lifted himself slowly to his feet, sighing wearily.

"You will not go without trying a measure of our last run?" invited Orugh, on his feet also.

"I will not try it, Orugh, and thank you. It might not sit well on what is before it. Come round to-morrow, Cond, and I will have the new blend ready."

"I may not be round to-morrow, Ager," answered Cond quietly.

When Ager had ridden off the five men sat still for a while and said nothing. The death of Urnaul had brought sadness to his kin, but accustomed as they were—as all men were—to swords and death, there was no great bitterness of anger or vengeance in them. Urnaul had been a likeable man in his own home, but the road he had chosen had dared Death at every turn, and Death, at last, had grown tired of being dared. Urnaul had found his only peace. His certain fate had overtaken him. Let him rest.

But though Urnaul had found his only peace, he had left no peace behind him. He had left a challenge on their hands that no manly men, at that time, could ignore. Baravais and Rem and all The Ser would know of that challenge, and would want to see how the answer came; and to four of the men there in the porch only one answer was possible.

They sat there thinking their own thoughts, and, beyond a doubt, four of them thought alike. Four pairs of eyes were turned on the hunched shoulders of Delgaun. He was the oldest, and he was full-brother to Urnaul. He had the first right to speak and do. They waited for him; but Delgaun sat tongueless, moveless, still as a stone, thinking his own thoughts. Their eyes could not move him.

Cond, at last, leaped to his feet.

" Let it be ! " he cried fiercely, as if someone had been speaking. " I am glad. In my bones I always knew that I would look over the hilt at Fergus of Running Water."

" That is Delgaun's right—and mine," protested Maur. We are Urnaul's full-brothers."

"It is Delgaun's right if he claims it," agreed
Cond. "But he is no swordsman, and I am. I
will take the sword."

Maur sprang to his feet.

"No! I am Urnaul's full-brother too. I will
take the sword. It is my right."

"Speak of your rights a year from now when
you are a man," said Cond, and pushed him force-
fully down on the bench.

Delgaun came alive at last, but quietly. He
rose slowly to his feet and faced round on Cond.
His dark, strong-boned face was grave and firmly
set. A man entirely controlled by his own reasoning will.

"This sword-fighting is all folly," he said,
"and even death is not the end of it—except for
Urnaul. It is the end he chose." He put a hand
on Cond's shoulder. "Cond, brother, can I say
nothing that will stay you?"

"Only one thing, Delgaun, since the first right
is yours."

"And that thing I will not say." Delgaun's
voice deepened. "I will not fight. I dare not
fight. I will play no games with Fate that has used
me hardly." He looked over Cond's shoulder at
his father, and hopelessness was in the appeal of
his voice. "Orugh, my father, will you not set
your face against this folly of going out with that
sword?"

Orugh touched the hilt on his lap.

"I will not break a custom or make a custom," he said. "This is Urnaul's sword. I made it. Swordmaking is my trade."

"Ye are tied by custom. Let it be so!" Delgaun's hand firmed on Cond's shoulder. "Listen, Cond! I will not go, and you will. You are a good swordsman, better than Urnaul because of your speed. Remember what Maur said. Keep the blades engaged, using your wrist and your thigh, until you are ready to strike. You will remember that?"

"I will remember it," said Cond, the corner of his mouth lifting, "but it is easy to be skilled no sword in your hand."

He drew his shoulder away from Delgaun's grasp, turned, and took the sword from his father's knees. He looked over the hilt of it at Flann, and his voice was as derisive as Flann's own.

"If this sword comes back, Flann, you are to forget with all your might that Cond was your full-brother."

"I will start doing that now, Cond," promised Flann, satire to the end; "but, if memory is too strong for me, there is Maur's trick of fence to fall back upon."

"It will not help you, Flann," Maur told him, and he was prophetic without knowing it.

## CHAPTER III.

### *The Sword Comes Home Again.*

A WEEK after the mid-winter festival the sword came home again.

Cond did not bring it. Cond lay dead in Alder Hollow of The Ser, and Fergus of Running Water was alive though wounded and wounded again. Everywhere men talked of the bloody long-drawn-out battle ; how the swords gripped each other as with hands ; how Fergus, tense like forged iron, light like a leaf, tore his blade free time and again, to draw blood ; how Cond slowly weakened and at last fell ; and how Fergus fell at his side, struggled up for the finishing blow, and fell again.

The sword came back to Orugh and his three sons, and, as before, a message came with it.

" I send back the sword," it ran. " Cond was a good man, but ye will need to send a better."

" Fergus the killer will not be sent that one—or any one," declared Flann with conviction.

And Delgaun, placing his hands on his half-brother's shoulders, besought him.

37

" Hold you by that, Flann, for killing is an unmanly thing."

" Good man, yourself, Delgaun ! " said Flann. " I will hold by it."

" You can hold by it for yourself," cried young Maur, " but I have my rights too."

" You are not yet a man," said his father quickly.

Flann looked at Delgaun, the satiric quirk to his mouth.

" He will be amongst the men this coming spring. What will you do then, Delgaun, with your cow's calf ? "

" I will not be driven."

" You are hard to drive. That is what you mean. Maur is a young fool, we know, but we would not like to waste him. What is that trick of fence he had for us ? "

" You know it," Maur told him sourly, " but you need skill for it."

" That is the end of it for me," said Flann definitely.

But next morning Flann rose with the first light, dressed himself for the road, and slung the long sword over his shoulder ; and his face and his voice mocked himself and the world.

" The truth is with you, Delgaun, but I cannot face it. I have tried, and I have tried hard, but I cannot forget that I am Cond's brother—and

Maur's brother too. There is no need to say anything to me."

He went out of the house without another word, and Delgaun covered his face with his hands.

"I find that I am fond of Flann," he whispered.

"It will be my turn next," cried Maur, throwing back his supple young shoulders.

Orugh, the father, groaned deeply at the fireside.

"It is a hard thing to be a father."

Delgaun turned on him, and their eyes met; and there was the same fear in both their eyes.

"A hard thing to be a father!" rasped Delgaun harshly. "You know that at last, old man. Fate is cutting close to the bone for you. Who put the sword in her hands? Let her cut, then! I will put no hand to any sword."

## CHAPTER IV.

### *And Still the Sword Comes Home.*

FLANN brought the sword back himself.

It was a brisk, clear evening after a sunny day of springtide, and on the open hearth of Orugh's house a fire of logs flamed brightly, filling the cavernous room with a ruddy, homely, heart-easing glow, glistening on the resinous black rafters of the low-pitched roof, gleaming on bronze shields and on the hilts of iron swords, setting grotesque shadows dancing on the lime-white walls.

Orugh and his two sons, Delgaun and Maur, sat before the hearth, their faces withdrawn and serious, the high lights defining the bosses of cheek and jaw. The silence that had grown with the months weighted upon them. Even Maur had lost his ready tongue.

Somewhere nearby a hound barked, and Maur turned a listening ear towards the door. In a little while a step sounded on the boards of the porch, and a man pushed the door open to the wan light of evening. That man was Flann.

The three figures about the fire stirred, made a move as if to rise, and then sat very still.

"You are welcome home, son," said the father gravely.

"Maybe I am, Orugh." Flann's voice, at any rate, had not lost its satiric trick.

He walked on feet not too certain to the fireside, and Delgaun pulled a straw hassock behind his knees. But he did not sit down.

"You will eat, brother," said Maur, and made to rise to his feet. But Flann's left hand on his shoulder held him.

"Not yet, man-grown. There is something to be said,"

Flann stood looking down at the flames, his cheek-bones strongly lit, and his long hollow cheeks in shadow. The hilt of the long sword stood up above his left shoulder, and his right arm was slung in a silken scarf across his breast.

"Sit you, son," Orugh urged.

Flann drew his arm from the sling and thrust it into the light of the fire.

"Fergus of Running Water did that to me."

There was a white rag on the stump of the forearm where a hand had been.

The three men drew in their breaths.

"He did it neatly," said Flann.

"I will fashion a bronze hook for you," said steady old Orugh, steady-voiced.

"It is what you would say, my father, but is it all you have to say?" Flann laughed bitterly. "Why do you not ask: 'Is Fergus dead, and where is Alor?' Alor is in her own house in Alder Hollow, and Fergus is not dead. Fergus is far from death, and all his wounds healed, but none of them are wounds of my dealing. He refused to kill a man who had no skill. But he did that to me. 'Take your sword home, you will not need it any more,' he said. 'Take your sword home, and tell Orugh to make a sickle of it.' That was the message this time."

Flann sat down, and carefully returned his maimed arm to its sling.

But Maur was on his feet, hands clashing together, head thrown high, body like the whip of a lance.

"A sickle it will be," he cried. "A sickle of death and I wielding it! Look at me! I am a man grown, and my right is my own. All this winter I have practised swording, and there is not a man in Long Baravais can touch me, point or edge. I will take the sword." He put his hand to the hilt above Flann's shoulder. "Are ye listening to me? I will take the sword."

"Make a song of it," Flann said.

"The song will come later. Let the sword sing and I be silent."

" It has come at last, Orugh." Delgaun spoke deeply, head down, and eyes still on the fire.

" It has come," agreed Orugh. " A hard thing to be a father ! "

" A hard thing to be unhappy—that is what you mean, old man." And Delgaun's sombre voice, finding tongue, went on reasoning to itself, and all listened. " Unhappiness comes always, but it comes harder on the young. I was once young that am not yet old. And I know, too, that unhappiness does not come hard on the old. Orugh is old, his high deeds and hot desires behind him, laughter easy to him, and tears easy, and all his yesterdays only a dream. I know all that, and yet, and yet ! " He lifted his head, leant forward to the old man, and looked close into his face. " And yet, foolish that I am, I would do anything in my power to keep this last unhappiness from you, my father."

" You are no fighting man, Delgaun. You can do nothing."

" Nothing ! I know that. I can do nothing, for no man can escape his destiny. At last I know that. A man I loved lost his life, and one his right hand, and another, for all that he is skilled, may die also, in his finest youth. And still reason tells me with all its voice to avoid touching hilt of sword."

" You would only die too, Delgaun."

43

"Die! That is easy. It could be that the choice of death is the best choice. Urnaul dead, Cond dead, Flann maimed, let Maur die too, and then Delgaun! Will you hobble out with the sword then, old man?"

"I will go as far as I am able. It is the custom."

"That is your answer," said Delgaun, and rose to his feet. He went to the open door and stood looking out over the marshes of Rem, grey-green in the gloaming, starred with splashes of water glistening like cold steel in the afterlight. After a while he spoke, and the heavy, lonely timbre of his voice had an undertone of bitter revolt and terrible despair.

"I used make songs too, Maur, and I was one of your wandering men of Baravais. The wastes of Rem before my eyes, the high calling of the curlew, the flighting of the duck, the trump of the wild geese in the dark of the morning, put restlessness on me, set my feet on roads across the world—across all the world. . . . But at the end, when I thought I could remember nothing but my own bitterness, I remembered the russet green of the bearded rushes, the ruddy green of the marsh grasses, the emerald green of Rem ribbon; I remembered the little pools shimmering in the sun, shivering in the wind, silvering in the light of the gloaming; I remembered the lonely calling of the curlew, the long necks of the ducks, the wedge of the geese voyaging northwards ; I remembered all the sights and sounds, and the clean salt air of the sea. So was I drawn home to Long Baravais, to my father's quiet house, to hear again the shore birds cry and see the gold bar of the sea under the setting sun ; to sit after the day and drink our father's wine and talk of the mysteries that have no solving, and, when my time came, quietly to die, and sleep—and sleep—and sleep ; and sleep would be the best of all."

He paused, and Flann spoke in a strangely gentle voice.

"Maur could never sing like you, Delgaun. Oh ! but I am glad that I am home."

"Rest you, my brother—it is your due—but I am far from sleep. Reason is dead in me, and the Baravais wander drouth has to be slaked again. My eyes are weary of the marshes of Rem ; the salt air has grown bitter in my blood ; my father's wine, that inspired me yesterday, is grown sour to-day. Let it be so ! "

He turned and strode across to his father's side.

"Orugh, who makes swords, I will take to the road with your son Maur."

"The sword, Delgaun ? " Orugh put to him.

"I will take no sword,"

"I will take the sword," cried Maur, "and in our own time bring it down on The Ser and on Fergus."

He was again the vital, seeking youth, all the gloom of winter shed from him.

"Tell me, Flann," he enquired eagerly, "did you see Alor?"

"I saw her."

"What is she like?"

"She is a woman with red hair, and she stays in a man's mind."

"Is that all?"

"It is enough." Again Flann thrust out his maimed arm. "She salved that for me. She minded me in a dry fever, and cooled my brow with the coolness of her hand. This is her scarf, and that is her last bandage. She is kind—she is not wicked." He laughed unhappily. "Look ye! If I could grow a hand on that stump I would sally out again, and again try Fergus with Maur's trick. That is the kind of woman Alor is."

"I will judge her for myself," proclaimed Maur.

"Let it be so," said Delgaun.

## CHAPTER V.

### The Wandering Men.

DELGAUN and Maur went many steps on the roads
that Delgaun had known of old. Delgaun curbed
Maur's impatience, and insisted that there was no
hurry, since the end of the road they were on was
sure and might be the end of all roads. So they
swung well away from the high plain of The Ser,
and went northwards on the skirts of the mountains,
resting and loitering in the pleasant peopled valleys
that splayed out from the trunks of the ridges.

In time they came to the grey Northern Sea, and
crossed over to the grassy downs and wooded
wealds of Britain, and partook of the famous
metheglin that the equable friendly people poured
for them so plentifully. And from Britain they went
west among the hill tribes of the Cymri, where there
was much singing, and where Maur recited his own
verse, and was happy when harpers plucked
harmonies to his voice.

From an island of oak woods and druids they took
passage in a Phoenician sailed-boat going to Inver

Colpa in Erin for a cargo of copper, and from Inver Colpa they went inland thirty miles to the royal palace of Tara, where Conaire had just been crowned High King on the Stone of Destiny. Conaire was a youth but not a weakling. He suffered under the burden of nine tribal tabus, and under the greater burden of four foster-brothers. But he paid little heed to his tabus, held his brothers on a tight rein, and kept the peace of Erin intact in his two strong young hands.

They went north then to Emain Macha in Ulster where Conchobar was king. They found Ulster desolate. The Red Branch Knights were scattered and their hostel burned ; the three great sons of Usna were dead, and Conchobar had seen golden Deirdre die on the breast of Naoise that he had slain. "Alor is like that dead one," said Maur. All manly men shunned Conchobar ; Fergus had gone into Connacht to be made love to by Maeve the Queen ; the mighty Cuchulain had made a reiving expedition to Cumbria ; Conall Cernach had betaken himself to the dun of his father, Amorgen.

The two brothers did not stay long in that Ulster of gloom, but crossed the narrow Waters of Moyle to the Pictish kingdom of Strathclyde, where they had to move circumspectly, for though the people were hospitable their priests had an unpleasant habit, at certain sacred seasons, of sacrificing a

48

man—a stranger preferably—on tables of stone within an oak grove.

From the Clyde they went amongst savage mountains to the Kingdom of Dalriada, ruled by big, merry, blonde-red fighting men who used the throwing spear and the short bronze sword. When these merry smiters saw the sword behind Maur's shoulder they wondered at the length of it and the metal of it—they had never seen iron—and one or two wondered if Maur could use it. But Delgaun explained that Maur had a challenge on his hands, and that the sword was sacred to that challenge. After that they were treated like brothers.

From Dalriada they went through even more savage mountains, and made a three days' march up a great glen, with three long lakes for a floor, to another Pictish town where Broad River met the tide of a sea fiord. This was the strongest Pictish kingdom in Alba, and ruled all the north, and ruled it well, so that the brothers were able to move in safety to the very Drum of Cait at the end of all things.

Beyond Cait, to the Pole, ran wastes of green ocean out of which stood tall islands with immense prows turned westwards to the beat of the sea. They were the only prows in that desert of water. Many centuries had yet to pass before the coming of the high-prowed long-ships manned by blond savages who were to kill and feast and make love so incontinently and without grace.

But, alas! Delgaun could not forever keep edging away from the thing that drew Maur. Southwards they had to turn and southwards go, and again they had to cross over the Northern Sea in a Roman trireme carrying tribute from South Britain. And at last, and at long last, they again saw, far in the south, the smoky blue ramparts that hedged and upheld The Ser. In three days they were toiling over the Pass of Paps, and in two days more were far out into the vastness of the high plain.

It was hereabouts that Maur began to suffer small moods of depression and even more tell-tale little fits of gaiety. He was no coward, but he was highly strung.

The story must be knit closer now.

Behold them, then, of a fine morning in late summer, on their final march. Behind them the stupendous plain of The Ser spread itself out to where, far and far away, loomed the blue ridge of the mountains ; and the same weary sweep of plain spread away in front of them, slowly lifting its grey-green like the sea until, like the sea, it rolled starkly in a dead straight line over the horizon beyond which were, not mountains, but serene white towers of clouds lifting out of the void beyond the world's edge. Far-flung though that plain was, the immense arch of the sky did not come down to meet the horizon, but curved and swooped far and untellably far beyond it, so that the towering white clouds seemed to be in the near foreground, and the plain, by contrast, no more than a palm's breadth balanced in the void. An imaginative man might have a fear that this plot of earth would at any moment reel and topple and fall forever through that vacant void.

Maur was in a good mood this morning. He did not walk as if on the brink of the void. He was not what, in fact, he was : a mere speck crawling on an overawed cowering spread of plain that swept briefly to the horizon and rolled over into the depths of the sky. In his own mind he towered into that sky and looked abroad over worlds, for he was at one with the sky and mountain and cloud, and the austere morning light he evolved out of himself.

Maur wore a saffron-orange cloak over his green-girdled white tunic, and aside on his jaunty head clung a green cap with an orange flap falling to his shoulders. At one hip swung a small leather satchel that clinked as he walked, and over his left shoulder stood the chased hilt of the long sword. As was his habit, he did not seem to be walking of any set purpose. He strolled, he loitered, he paused, and hurried to overtake the steadily pacing Delgaun, who smiled at him tolerantly and went on pacing ; he gazed narrow-lidded into the abyss of the sky, wide-eyed at the cloud-mountains beyond the world, frowningly at the sun-withered grass about his feet ; he whispered words to himself, whistled the bar of a tune, intoned the verse of a song. Evidently the song was his own, for he smiled with some vanity, recited the verse to flavour it, changed a word or two, and again intoned :

> " Let Death my footsteps dog
> With threat of Pain thereafter,
> I season Life with Love,
> And Love with Laughter."

He was not thinking of death at all, nor of love.

" I like that bit," said he.

Sober Delgaun, never changing his easy, long-thighed stride, shook his head and smiled.

" If Flann were here with us he would call it a bad song, and, besides, not a true one."

" How so, Delgaun ? "

" He would say that Death is only the welcomer at the end of pleasant roads or hard ones, and that Pain has no meaning where there is no beginning or no end. And he would say that Love, from what he has seen of it, has many attributes but that Laughter is not one of them. Try it again, boy."

" Maybe he would be right," said Maur, but doubtfully. " He sometimes is."

" He is sometimes wrong, too, but not so often."

Maur paused, frowned, looked at his sandalled

feet, and grew vacant-eyed with the inner travail of creation. There was never a better companion on any road, for though he was wayward and moody, he was sound as a bell at bottom.

Delgaun went pacing steadily onward, a sober man in a brown cloak over a crotal brown tunic. He was a man of good height, carrying little flesh on his big bones, but showing no signs of great strength or urgent speed ; just an ordinary tall man of enduring toughness, unduly long in the thigh, perhaps. He had a blue-shaven, strongly-moulded, grave face, black hair cut straight above black bar of brow, and eyes purple-blue as deep-sea water. A sober man, with all the fires quenched in him. His only weapon was a smooth long staff of seasoned ash, double-horned with iron.

Delgaun strode on, lifted up a few feet of slope that wound almost unnoticeably across the plain, and came to a dead halt.

" This might be the end of our road," said he.

He was looking down into a small valley.

That valley was one of the secrets so well hidden in the vastness of The Ser. That great plain seemed everywhere to flow up and over the horizon desolate and austere, with nothing amove but the cloud shadows or the wind or the grass leaning with the wind, with no shelter where one might cower away from the uncaring void ; yet all across its vastness it was seamed with little hollows such as this : a narrow, shallow, verdant, pleasant, winding valley, with a stream loitering and hasting, a cluster of shielings about a wimpling ford, hand-tilled gardens on one slope, and, on the other, terraced vineyards facing the sun.

A hundred long down-hill paces below Delgaun, and on the near side of the stream, two score or more people were loosely congregated. They were all men, a varicoloured group reclining at scattered ease about a circular clay-stamped exercise ground, eating the forenoon meal, and idly watching two boys playing at wrestling. Above the ford a hand-railed plank made a foot-bridge, and at each side of it a cluster of low grass-thatched houses sheltered under the slopes. Here and there between the houses bare-legged children were at play ; and bright-kirtled women sat about the doors.

" Here, brother ! " Delgaun called to Maur striding up the rise. " I see our morning meal in front of us."

" Eating is more profitable than bad song-making," said Maur sadly. He came to Delgaun's side and looked with surprise into the valley. " What place is this ? "

" It might be the place we are looking for."

Maur glanced quickly at Delgaun and controlled his voice. " It is time we came to it."

" Do not name your name until you are asked," said Delgaun. " Come ! "

He threw his head up in some final abandoned gesture of acceptance, and strode down over the brink of the valley. Maur followed him.

And then, over the immensity of the plain, there was nothing but grey-green grass undulating smoothly in the breeze, and cloud shadows sliding smoothly under the sun, and a terrible uncaring awareness.

Down in the valley the whole atmosphere underwent some subtle change : quiet not aloof, secure not uncaring, serene not austere, restful not immobile. There was the comfortable, sheltered feeling of a fire-lit house with the wind outside. Outlanders held that the people of The Ser moved like moles within their sheltered burrows, hiding away from the weariness of the plain and the eternal yawn of the horizon. This was not all true. The people of The Ser were indeed awed by the plain, but they loved it. They had a custom of creeping up to the rim of their valleys when the red ball of the sun they worshipped was going down beyond the far-flung horizon. They crouched on the brink awed by the immensity, feeling more intensely their own sheltered security, appreciating more keenly the kindliness of the darkening hollow behind them, reassuring themselves of the even, if not high, level they had won from life. That was The Ser and the magic of it.

Delgaun came to the margin of the group about the exercise ring, and saluted.

" Good day to the good work ! "

" Welcome over the brink, " said an elderly man. " Sit in and eat with us."

They made room for the brothers, served them with brown bread and a blue-veined cheese, and moved a jug of dark wine near their hands.

These men of The Ser were short in stature, sallow of skin, and strong-bearded. They wore short tunics and long trews of brightly-dyed linen, and carried no weapons. Maur did not like them. He did not like their subdued, almost cowed, secretive eyes. He felt that there was some secret ugly thing in their minds, something that they gloated over and were ashamed of ; and he noted how their eyes, careless of Delgaun and his staff of ash, came furtively to the hilt of the long sword above his own left shoulder.

They were interested in the news of the world outside The Ser, and Maur suspected their reason. Maur was a good talker and Delgaun let him talk. He talked to them of the easy-going men of Britain and their famous mead, of the singing men of Cymri, of the tragedy of Deirdre, of the Scots who ate flesh only and drank a terrific liquor made of fire, of the Picts who had evolved a power of darkness calling for the sacrifice of blood.

"A barbarous people all," commented the elderly man who had elected himself forespeaker.

"If you mean forthright, yes. You find barbarity all places—even in The Ser."

The man's shoulders stirred, and, after a time he put the question at the back of his mind—of all their minds.

"Did ye happen to come through Long Baravais?"

"We are going that way," Maur told him carelessly. "Is it noted for anything?"

"It used have great sword-fighters in it."

"But not know?"

"A man of The Ser killed most of them."

"Who is he?"

"Fergus of Running Water."

"Is this Running Water?"

"No. Running Water is a mile downstream."

"What place is this, then?"

"This is Alder Hollow."

"Ah!" said Maur. "Is not this the place where the woman named Alor lived?"

"She lives here yet," answered the forespeaker proudly, and gestured with a hand.

Some distance—two long spear-casts—up the valley, a wooden-stooped hut sheltered under a huge leaning alder on the brink of the stream; and a woman in a sky-blue robe sat on the crutch of a root, her shoulder against the trunk of the tree.

" That is Alor," said the forespeaker. " The woman with red hair."

" I will look at it," said Maur briefly, and lifted lightly to his feet. Without another word he strode away up the valley.

Delgaun rose to his feet too, but more heavily.

" May your store increase," he gave the valediction.

But, before he could move after Maur, the forespeaker put him a quick question.

" Who is that young man ? "

Delgaun hesitated and answered.

" Bread broken, you will know. He is Maur, the son of Orugh, the swordmaker."

" Indeed ! The brother of Urnaul—— ? "

" And of Cond. That is who he is."

" And who are you ? "

" I have no name now. But you may find out."

And Delgaun moved away, walking heavily, his staff of ash helping his slow feet.

His back was scarcely turned before the forespeaker gave a quick, whispered order, and a youth, slipping away from the ring, ran with all his speed down the course of the stream. Delgaun heard the pelt of the flying feet, and shook his heavy head.

" The men of The Ser are more barbarous than the Scots."

# CHAPTER VI.

## *The Woman Alor.*

ALOR saw the two men coming, one behind the other, but already she had seen them come over the brink.

She had been sitting as she sat now, a shoulder against the alder, her eyes vacant in dream, her fingers crumbling brown bread, her ears half-hearing the quiet water of the pool, rippled by the eddy of a trout, lap-lap softly against the over-hang of the bank, when something—chance or fore-boding—made her lift eyes to the rim of the valley ; and there, on the very brink, a man stood on wide-planted feet, a triangle of sky showing between his legs. That triangle of sky and some trick of eyesight made the man tower colossal into the blue. One far-reaching arm thrown out, as it were, across universes and spiral nebulae, held down little Earth under the point of a staff, and his vast and brooding head was set forward towards her through deeps of air. She saw him throw up that massive head, the promontory of his jaw against the sky, and take one mighty stride over the rim of the valley, and then she saw that he was no more than a tall man; but in all her after days her outstanding memory of that tall man was as she had first seen him, a Colossus filling the void, a portent that, in one long stride, had assumed the littleness of a man to deal with men and with her.

Here, now, were the two men coming to see her. Well! many men had come to see Alor—and many of them would never see anything any more. She could not help that. It had, by a fable in men's minds, gone beyond her help. The tall man she had seen as a portent came, on the prop of a staff, behind a supple youth. Supple as a wand, strong as a lance, dusky and beautiful, and with the cross of a hilt above his left shoulder! Poor foolish men looking death one at another over the hilt of a sword, for the love of death or the love of woman!

The youth stopped before her, and gave her the woman's salute, hand to brow. She did not incline her head in return, but kept her eyes on him calmly. His voice rang.

"I am Maur, the brother of Urnaul."

The calmness of her remained calm as still water.

"Then you are also the brother of Cond and Flann?" Her voice, though she had red hair, was low in pitch like a man's voice, but not harsh.

"That is who I am," said Maur.

" And who is this man ? "

Delgaun had come to Maur's side, and she looked at him, hiding her interest ; and Delgaun looked at her, his eyes steadfast in a steadfast dark face.

" He is Delgaun, my brother," Maur told her.

" Urnaul used speak of Delgaun, who never carried sword. How wise, Delgaun ! "

" Men speak of Alor, too," said Maur. " Men speak of her in all the valleys and on all the hills."

" Men are always at the speaking. It is a refuge of theirs. You will tell me if Flann's arm is healed ? "

" It is healed, but he has another wound that will not heal."

" I do not believe in that kind of wound. Will ye break bread ? "

" We have eaten."

" Sit ye, then. Ye will not sit long. A messenger has gone with evil gloating in his mind."

" She is the calm one," said Maur to himself, and sat on the edge of the porch.

Delgaun stayed where he was, planted firmly on the ground, leaning a little forward on his staff, his hands resting in the curve of the double-horn, and his chin over his folded hands. He had spoken no word yet.

She turned a little to face between them, her shoulder still against the tree-trunk, her eyes calm, almost weary, surely sad, all emotion hidden away behind her calm and warm beauty—for beautiful she was at least. The water gurgled softly somewhere nearby; a small breeze moved in the dark-green leaves of the alder, stirred in the lustre of her hair, died away into the quietness that was all about them.

But there was no quietness in Maur, though he had lost his tongue all of a sudden. There was a ferment in his mind already, and the beginning of a new song—his great song. Alor was beautiful—indeed she was beautiful—sitting there so still, but she was not at all the Alor he had pictured in his mind's eye. That one had been a cold virgin, sculptured out of pale marble, with a flame for crown. But this one was a girl, and young—troublingly lovely—coloured, warm, alluring—delicate, rich, glowing, live, human flesh and blood . . . Her sky-blue robe was alive with the life inside it . . . And her eyes! Her eyes in some lights would be grey, and in some dark, and in some touched with green, and in no light at all touched with blue—and all the time they would be shot through with an inner lustre. A birch tree after rain, her perfume! A pool sun-lit in basalt to cool the thirst that would thirst again! Man had no weapon against her. Reason to fatalism, coldness to surrender, thought to dreaming, man had no weapon against her . . . Such was a little of the yeasty ferment out of which Maur would distil his great song.

But sober Delgaun of Long Baravais, that reasoning, steadfast man, told himself that he was looking at no more than a medium-tall, red-haired, clear-skinned, grey-eyed, shapely young woman, who had a woman's appeal to the man's senses, and added to her charm a bold calmness that might be more dangerous than fire.

The silence held for a while, and then Alor broke it.

"When Delgaun is still, as he is now, I know him for Urnaul's brother."

"I am Urnaul's brother in more ways than one," said Delgaun's deep voice. "Does Alor see that?"

"Alor does not see that, but it might be so."

"You should see that, who see all things," declared Maur, no longer tongue-tied. He consumed her with his poet's eyes. "About you I was wrong, Alor. I limned a picture of you and called you, 'Woman-without-Mercy.' I was wrong, but you are still without mercy."

"I am only a woman." Alor laughed sadly and mockingly. "Tell me the wiles I use?"

"You use no wiles, who are all wile despite you."

"I think that Maur is a maker of songs."

"I will make a song about Alor."

"It will not be a true one."

"It will be the best I can do."

"It will not be true, nevertheless."

"There will be in it the death of Urnaul and Cond."

"I did not bring them death."

"Yet they are dead. There will be in it the seeking of a woman who thought she could find love."

"That is better, but love does its own seeking and I shall know it when it finds me. Put that in your song."

"I will put that love has found only death by you."

"That is not true, but you will not believe me." A trace of anger ruffled her calm, and that pleased Maur.

"Why are you blind? This is what you must put in your song. All seeking, even that of love, is folly, and Alor has found no true man in all the world."

"There as Urnaul."

"He is dead, and love did not kill him."

"And Cond?"

"Cond I did not know. Urnaul killed him."

"Urnaul?"

"As sure as with sword, and he maimed Flann, who is the best man that I have met. Flann has a soft heart—he will suffer always."

Delgaun moved his head in assent, and his eyes and his mind were intent on her.

"Fergus of Running Water is not dead," went on Maur at his own seeking.

"He is no man of mine."

"He will be my man this very day," declared Maur boldly.

"Be not boasting. I fear that your great song will never come to its singing."

Her voice carried the very note of doom. His dreamer's eyes widened on her, and he saw himself broken away from life in uncaring death. O Death! was he to find that uncaring one this day, and never see Alor again—his great song unsung?

"You have no fear," he almost whispered, and found nothing else to say. Silence drove down on him.

"I do not fear you or Fergus," said Alor, "but I could fear the man at your side."

Maur looked up at Delgaun, but Delgaun was no longer looking at Alor. He gazed at the ground over his folded hands, and his strongly-moulded face was not fearsome. Maur, who loved him and obeyed him out of love, could not imagine anyone fearing this sober, reasoning brother.

The heavy ruminative voice of Delgaun began speaking as if to himself.

"I listened to Alor playing at words with Maur,

but her words were not all play. Her words I
remember as in a dream I had long ago, when I
understood them as Maur does now.'' He lifted
his eyes to hers. '' Could I speak to you, Alor ? ''

She sat up and faced him directly, and her
interest was not hidden.

'' I will answer as best I can.''

'' Urnaul was a likeable man ? '' he began in his
reasoning way.

'' And I liked Urnaul,'' Alor answered the
implied question.

'' Urnaul was my mother's son,'' he went on.
'' He was quiet like she was, and when he was little
he used follow me everywhere, holding my finger
and trusting me as once men trusted the old gods.
And Alor liked the brother that I loved ? ''

'' I liked him, Delgaun.''

'' But he loved, Alor ? ''

'' Are you sure that he loved me, Delgaun ? ''

'' It is the thing that troubles me, Alor. You
will tell me ? ''

'' I think that you understand, dark man,
however knowledge came to you. Why is your
name not in the mouths of men ? ''

Delgaun did not answer that, but held to his
question.

'' You will tell me, Alor, the thing that was in
Urnaul's heart ? ''

'' I will tell you, because I must. Because I am

afraid." She leant to him, her hands clasped on her knees, and her face and voice alive and urgent. "Know you, there are two men that I—that no woman can hold. One of them is the man that kills—the Killer. Do you know that, Delgaun?"

"I knew it."

"Then you will know that the love of killing grows on what is shed. The Killer has only one passion, and he goes on killing till he himself is the kill. In the beginning he might love a woman, but in a little while no beauty will move him, no love sweep him, no passion tear him, for he has a thirst that no wine of love can quench, a passion that will share nothing with the love of woman or the love of wine, or the love of anything but the game of death in the clash of swords. You know that, Delgaun?"

"I knew it."

"You said Urnaul loved me. Urnaul of Rem, the lover! Urnaul of Rem was only a Killer. A Killer! like Fergus of Running Water, Cuchulain the Hound, that terrible Stone-Face of Mussoul."

"That man, too," agreed Delgaun.

"Look you, Delgaun! Once I thought I loved Urnaul. Indeed, I am wicked! I thought I loved many men, and grew to hate them all—except Urnaul. Urnaul I liked always, and had come to think that that liking was what the first high dreaming of love must sink to always. When I saw the tides sweeping him I asked him to take me to his father's house.  He would—to-morrow, the day after, in one moon, when the year turned, after a last challenge.  And the last challenge came, and he died.  I am only a fable, Delgaun.  Do not blame me or anyone for the death of Urnaul."

" I do not blame you, Alor."

Her face flushed and lit into soft loveliness, and her eyes, grown darker, met and held his.

" You know that I speak the truth ? "

" I know it too well."

" I am glad.  I was afraid.  What would you do, Delgaun, if you did not believe ? "

" I came here to kill you," he said simply.

" I was afraid.  And I am not afraid."  She opened her hands to him in a hopeless yet moving way.  " I feel death near me these many days."

" It is very near you."

" I see it in the eyes of the men of The Ser watching me."

" Before this day is out," said Delgaun, " it may be closer still, and I the bringer."

Maur stared at his brother as if he were seeing him for the first time.  There was some deep, strong current in his speech that he could not follow, and that Alor could.  But, suddenly, Maur had a thought that he could lay hold of, and he made a question of it.

" You said there were two men you—no woman—could hold, Alor.  Who is the second ? "

" You are the last man I would tell that to,"
answered Alor, and smiled at him.

At that instant a shadow fell on the grass
amongst them, and the three turned and looked at
the caster of the shadow.

" I am Fergus of Running Water," announced
the stranger.

# CHAPTER VII.

## *The Challenge of Fergus.*

FERGUS OF RUNNING WATER was the greatest swordsman in all the hollows of The Ser; no one in The Ser disputed that any longer. But one might wonder where in that slender body hid the force that must be mated with skill to make greatness. He was tall enough, but his leanness did not give an impression of speed or litheness. The sloping shoulders did not swing, and, as he walked in an odd, jerking, stiff-kneed strut, the line from the back of his head to his waist was as straight and as stiffly held as a bar of iron. His face showed no blood, but was one even colour of wood ashes; his eyes were small and pale and deep-set; and his hair thin and fine and flaxen. But though his body was stiffly held his face was not. It was forever smiling palely at some thought of his own, for, like all abnormal men, he was not wholly sane. Over his left shoulder he carried a sword, the twin of the one that Maur carried.

"I am Fergus of Running Water," he

announced in a light, high voice, and looked at the man carrying the sword. "I hear that you are Maur, the son of Orugh the swordmaker."

Maur stood to his feet and, though his heart was hard-beating to his throat, he made his words slow and even.

"I am Maur, the brother of Urnaul."

"The last of the litter!" He laughed. "Or has Orugh a boy with voice unbroken to send out before he crawls himself?"

Before Maur could think of a fitting answer, Fergus spoke again.

"And who is this sullen dark one who carries a staff of ash?"

Delgaun answered that question, and his heavy voice had now some brazen quality in it.

"I am a man that was dead. I have no name until you name it."

But Fergus only laughed—he laughed easily but without humour—and considered Delgaun out of fleering eyes

"I do not mind your name, but a man with a face like yours did not die easily. By whose sword?"

"A borrowed one," said Delgaun, and turned his shoulder away from him.

"You do not want to die twice, I see. A man with a staff of ash moves safely with Fergus." He turned back to Maur. "So you are Maur, the brother of Urnaul—and of Cond and Flann—and you carry the sword that three times I made sing to my own tune. Why did not Orugh make a sickle of it?"

"It will be a sickle of death," Maur told him, but not as hardily as he might.

"Why not? It was that in Urnaul's hand—till I came; and Cond had a trick or two as well. But Flann!—I warn you, stripling, that I am not often in the mood that gave Flann his maimed life."

And Maur, for the life of him, could not find words for a suitable retort.

"I take it that you are here to challenge me," Fergus went on lightly. "As you please. But you will note that I compel no man to fight me, though sword-fighting is the game I play with life, and I the player." He looked at Alor, and laughed mockingly. "It may be that their business is with you, Red One, and, for me, they are welcome. Urnaul made you his excuse for fight once or twice, but, myself, I seek no excuses. If your young cockerel wants a bout send him down to me in the ring."

He turned on his heel, still laughing, and strode off down the valley. In the play of words he had mastered them.

"That is the Killer," said Alor simply.

Maur nodded. "He was brief enough."

"But he kills slowly."

" This day I will do the killing." But, for the first time in his life, Maur was not sure of himself.

Alor was on her feet now and came between them. Her voice was at once appealing and hopeless.

" Is there nothing I can say will keep this sword in its sheath ? "

" I will listen to Alor," said Delgaun.

Maur's temper flared.

" No ! I will not listen. What am I here for ? "

He put his hand on the loop that held his sword, but Delgaun grasped his wrist before he could loose it.

" Patience, brother ! " he said firmly. " One must not choose death till there is no other road. Wait ye here for me ! "

He turned and went down the valley, walking heavily, his head down, and his staff helping his slow feet—an old and weary man.

Alor and Maur watched him go, and Maur could only wonder at this changed brother of his. Alor spoke at his side.

" You are afraid, Maur ? "

Maur considered that. " I am afraid, Alor," he admitted, " but since I cannot help it there is nothing I can do about it. The fear I have will make my hand cunning."

" I am beginning to like you, Maur."

" I will not be satisfied with liking," he said boldly, but not looking at her.

She did not heed that. "You need not be afraid," she told him.

"No?"

"Not if you obey Delgaun. You always obey him?"

"Everyone in Baravais does that—always."

"Always! Did he send Cond and Flann out to fight?"

"No. I was wrong. That time he pleaded with them, but there was the custom."

"Did he send you out?"

"He came with me."

"He loves you. You will obey him?"

"I will fight Fergus—I must fight Fergus," insisted Maur desperately.

"You will do what Delgaun tells you," insisted Alor.

Down by the ford, above the bridge, all the men of the hamlet, three score or so, were congregated round the brown, hard-beaten circle of the exercise ring; but, in addition, there were two score men from Running Water, and others, kites to the slaughter, were hurrying up by the bank of the stream. Fergus, leaning on the hilt of his sheathed sword, stood in the centre of the ring, and was in his best humour. The stage was his and he loved it.

"Here comes a hero with a staff," he cried.

74

" A fine weapon for a dead man who loves his second life—and it craven ! "

The men made room for Delgaun, and he stepped and halted within the margin of the ring. His face was serious and calm, and his voice was serious and calm too.

" I would speak to the men of Alder Hollow and Running Water ? "

There was a pause and then the forespeaker said briefly : " We listen."

" I have broken bread with you, and now, for your own sakes, and for the sake of Fergus, I would urge you with all my might to do one thing."

Fergus laughed high and clear, and patted the hilt of his sword.

" I do my urging with this—for its sake and for mine."

The forespeaker thrust a hand for silence.

" What would you urge, man-without-a-name ? "

" I would urge that you forbid Fergus to fight."

Again Fergus laughed his fleering laugh.

" Who would dare—— ? "

" Be silent, Fergus ! " shouted the forespeaker sternly, his hand again outflung. "If the people bid, you will obey, and if the people are driven to outlaw you, you will know it, and after that you will know nothing."

" Many will lack knowledge at the time I lack

it," Fergus taunted him. "Answer this careful fellow, old man!"

The forespeaker decided that there was nothing else to be done.

"Why must we forbid Fergus to fight, stranger?"

"The Killer shall not go on killing for the sake of killing. That is the law."

"We compel no man to fight Fergus, and Fergus does not fight except in challenge." A furtive murmur approved the forespeaker's words.

"Fergus ever cunningly arranges his own challenge, and kills and kills. Ye know it. The people outside The Ser hold ye to be wise. Will ye let the people know that the peace of Rome frets ye, that the solitude that surrounds ye under the bowl of the sky has, at last, made ye cruel? Do ye love blood?" He could not hide the taunt, the dislike, in his reasoning voice.

"We compel no man to fight Fergus," repeated the other stubbornly, and again the murmur went round the ring.

Delgaun looked slowly about the full circle, and there was contempt in his eyes, and contempt and despondency in his voice.

"Ye will not heed me. From the beginning I knew that ye would not heed me. I am too late. A secret lust rules ye. Ye are no longer wise."

"Are you our judge?"

"And I will judge ye," said Delgaun, and his voice hardened. "Ye have grown weary of the even level about ye and in ye. In secret ye love to be stirred by the sound of swords, the rending of wounds, the smell of blood. Ye are a dying people, and I warn ye that the lust ye suffer from is the beginning of the end. Look to your peace, ye fools, for soon the little rivers that run in all your hollows will sing mournfully in the silence, and the desolation that surrounds ye will have gathered ye in its arms. There! I have judged ye, and ye will not heed."

"A dead man giving tongue! Who heeds him?" mocked Fergus.

Slowly Delgaun again looked round the ring of subdued but obstinate faces, and his voice went harder. "Fools! Ye will not judge Fergus, your idol, and I dare ye to judge me. But there is one ye will judge as I have seen one judged. When Fergus is dead ye will judge Alor, putting a bandage, if need be, over your eyes that she be condemned."

A man of middle years whispered to his neighbour.

"That very thing was done the time Stone-Face killed the champion of Far Mussoul."

But the forespeaker, sensing the feeling about him, was as obstinate as ever.

"Whatever we may do to Alor or to Fergus, we

will be patient with you and compel you to nothing. If Fergus and your young swordsman fight they fight. Let them fight ! ''

'' Blood ye want ! Ye shall have it.'' Without another word Delgaun turned and strode out of the ring.

'' Send down your young smiter, old fellow,'' Fergus called after him, '' and I will show him the face of Death.''

# CHAPTER VIII.

### *The Dead Man Comes to Life.*

DELGAUN came to where Alor and Maur waited for him. Alor was standing now, lovely as an evening in high summer, and some excitement had warmed all her blood. Maur held the sheathed sword upright before him. His dusky young cheeks had blenched, but his jaw had a firm line.

" I am ready to kill him now, Delgaun."

Delgaun came close to him and looked into those young and stern eyes.

" Must Fergus die, then ? "

" He or I this day."

" Someone will die. Let it be so."

Delgaun turned from him to the stream, lifted up his staff, and ran his hand caressingly along the smooth length of it. Then he addressed it sternly sad.

" You were a fine companion on all our roads, and pleasant thoughts your aim. On many a mountain you held me up ; under my chin you whispered words of wisdom ; whistling in the air you kept tune to Maur's singing. Here now we part for all time. Go thou on a voyage of thine own!"

He slung it javelin-like into the water, where it dipped and sank and floated aslant to the tail of the pool where it balanced and swayed over a stone.

He faced round on Maur then, and took the long sword firmly out of his hands. The rigid face and glazed eyes Maur had never seen before.

"I am the blood-brother of Urnaul. You will do what I tell you."

To that brazen voice Maur made the only answer.

"What must I do,—Delgaun?" But was he Delgaun?

"You will go out of this hollow now—now—and southwards over the mountains to Long Baravais and your father's house. There you will stay till another hunger drives you."

"What will you do?"

"What is easy to me—the thing that the wolf in me howls to do, strange man that was my brother. I will do what Destiny has driven me to do since Urnaul died. And I know that I am lying when I say that I do it so that your father, Orugh, shall not lose the apple of his eye."

"Some day he shall lose it," said Alor softly.

Delgaun turned slowly to her, and she held herself from flinching before his terrible eyes.

"You are there, Alor, and my heart is empty of all desires but one. Yet I will be wise for a little while for your sake. Go you with Maur ! A woman, as you are, cannot long be safe anywhere, but even for one other hour you are not safe in this hollow of The Ser. Go you with Maur ! Your seeking was folly from the beginning and you know that now. Go to my father's house above the Rem. That pleasant, friendly house, not desolate, where you can hear the sea-birds' cry and see the gold bar of the sea under the setting sun. Listen to me ! I know that you will find peace there ; and you will spin your web, and drink my father's wine, and listen while men talk, and you will smile your woman's smile because you are wiser than all the men. And—yes !—in time you will find the father of your son ; and when your time comes you will sleep, and sleep, and sleep—and that will be best of all. Go you, Alor ! For I am only a dead man come to life."

Alor said no word ; but, all the time he had been speaking, her eyes, wide and grey, had remained drowned in his ; and slowly, slowly her eyes had darkened and a light had grown behind them.

But grim Delgaun turned his back on that light, and his hand wreathed round the hilt of the sword. The blade hissed out of its sheath and shone on him with a blue wickedness, and, suddenly, under some terrific power of wrist, made a double-loop in the air ; and the singing of it was thin and clear and full of madness.

" Thou patient one, thou ready one, thou singer of one song ! My father made you. He knew his work, and you know yours, and I know mine. You leap under my hand, and your voice is known to me."

The blade sheered and sang in tune to his words, and his voice was a brazen undertone to the singing of the blade.

He threw the sheath on the ground, and his glazed eyes went over shoulder to Alor and Maur.

" Be not here when I return."

He strode down the valley. He was no longer old, no longer weary. His long thighs thrust him forward with the unaware strength of the beast.

## CHAPTER IX.

### *Face of Stone.*

MEN flinched aside from Delgaun as he came, and he strode his way into the ring as if no one were there but Fergus.

"Come, brother!" lifted his brazen voice. "Two killers well met!"

Fergus did not laugh this time. He smiled palely, and his pale eyes began to grow yellow like a lion's.

"Well said, and well met, dead man! You may have a name after all."

"You will say it. Draw your sword!"

"Patience! You are in a hurry now, that came to life so slowly. What game were you playing?"

"The game of Life, and, now, Death."

"Death it will be. You played your game to the end, and I will play mine to the end, and in the end you will die and, again, not easily."

He drew his blade slowly. Three young men rushed forward to catch the sheath and cloak he threw, and wrestled for them as they bundled towards the margin of the ring. Fergus set himself and made two or three slow passes and then two or three lightning ones. He was a different man now. He moved forward and back on limber thigh muscles, his wrist was part of the hilt, his stiffness was the stiffness of the supple steel blade. He swung to Delgaun.

"I am ready, dead man," he said, and set himself on guard.

There were no more words and no ceremonies of battle. The men that crouched round the ring, subduedly gloating, were in another world. The two killers were alone in their own narrow tense one. They faced each other, intent, cat-like, cautious, crouching, stealthy, slowly circling, drawn together—closer—closer—deadly —one already doomed. Then the blades clanged and held ; and they held as if they had iron hands.

So they held and writhed, trying out the wrists behind them. Then Fergus started to fight. He hurled himself to the right, he hurled himself to the left, he drove forward on the full strain and leaped suddenly back like deer from snake ; but still the blades remained locked. Straining sinews stood out on forearms and on necks, bodies swayed and stiffened, bony knees bowed and trembled, muscles ridged flat on long thighs, feet that seemed to lift with feather ease met the ground with the stamp of iron, the edges of sandals scored the trodden clay of the ring. And always the blades remained locked. Fergus, for all his speed and sinew and lightness, could not tear his blade free.

" Let us try this way," he whispered.

He faced Delgaun, wrist against wrist, loin contending loin. The locked blades lifted with a smooth slowness into the air, hung there astrain, groaned and writhed, came down in a steep, sudden swoop to the very ground, and bent like a bow with a thin, grating double cry. A strong man using his strength might bend one of these blades into a half-circle, but, gnawing at each other here in Alder Hollow, they writhed on one another like hazel twigs.

Fergus found himself yielding the single stamping stride that he required for balance. He yielded it and Delgaun took the stride as it was yielded. The hilts came up shoulder high on the upper circle. Fergus took another stride for balance and Delgaun followed. A third and Delgaun strode with him. No blow had been struck. The blades remained locked.

And then Delgaun did a remarkable thing. He walked Fergus, slow pace after slow pace, round the full circuit of the ring. No matter how the blades writhed, near the ground or in the air, Fergus had to take one straining stride after another, and Delgaun paced easily after. It looked easy, but it was not. The braced loins, the ridged thighs showed that it was not; and as Delgaun paced the whole imprint of his sandals was bit deep into the packed clay of the ring. And, as he paced, slow words came out of a brazen throat.

" I am Urnaul—I am Cond—I am Flann—I am Maur—I am Delgaun—I am Fergus, too. There is another name. Name it, Fergus! Another name! Name it, Fergus! "

Fergus, holding the strain, never losing balance, not beaten, wary, waiting the chance that had never failed to come, looked yellow-eyed into Delgaun's face. That face, wiped clean of all human feeling and expression, was as rigid as a mask; the cheek-bones flat bosses of stone, nostrils flaring wings of porphyry, ridges of alabaster lining the promontory of jaw, eyes glazed harder than black marble.

"Another name! Name it, Fergus! "

" Stone-Face! " said Fergus.

" It is my name. And here is the one blow."

With the one shattering explosion of force that he had held ready Delgaun snapped his blade free; and Fergus suddenly loosed of the full strain came in a short stride, off-guard for a fraction of a second. No one there could follow the lightning flat half-sweep of Delgaun's blade. All that everyone saw was Fergus's head aleap in the air—leaping, falling, rolling, eyes still blazing yellow. And the body of Fergus planted on wide-set feet stood upright, swayed, crumpled, crashed, and his sword struck the earth. Fergus had found his only peace.

Then Delgaun swung full circle, and the men of Alder Hollow and Running Water shrank within themselves from that stone face and those stony eyes. And when he spoke, his voice came out of his throat as if that throat was brass, and, though not loud, it filled all the valley and the sky over it.

" I am Stone-Face. What man in The Ser will dare trouble Alor ? "

No man there uttered one small word.

# CHAPTER X.

## *The Staff of Peace.*

DELGAUN came to the hut by the alder tree. His order had been obeyed. There was no one there. He looked into the pool. His staff was gone, too. He sheathed his clean blade, hung it over his shoulder, and for a long time stood looking into the quiet flow of the water.

" To the rim of The Ser—I will guard ye from afar."

He spoke aloud as if addressing those within hearing, and went on brooding on the water. And the water gave a soft, remote, aloof little lap-lap under the over-hang of the bank. That strangely uncaring, heart-breaking sound made him throw up his head and look with wide-eyed hopelessness into the abyss of the sky.

" And then—and then—and then? I am nothing any more."

His voice boomed, and he went on staring unwinking into the deeps of the sky.

A deep and vital change had taken place in this

man Delgaun, and, in his own mind, that change should have stirred the heavens. But the void had not changed at all. The void remained austere and remote and uncaring; concerned not with Delgaun, nor with Life, nor with Love, nor with Death; concerned only with Nothing.

Delgaun, head down now, plodded slowly up the slope between the vineyards, where the grapes turning red and purple knew of their own fullness and their own death, and came over the brink to the desolation of the plain. There, as ever, the breeze blew forlornly across the leaning grass, and the cloud shadows ran smoothly under the sun. But a shadow at Delgaun's very feet stopped his feet dead, and brought his head up.

Alor was there. She stood facing him, alive, in her blue robe, upright like a spear, upright like the iron-horned staff she held against her breast with her two hands, emotion shimmering under the calm of her face, and her eyes darker than grey.

" It is all past now, Delgaun," she said in a quiet, low voice that was soothing yet anxious.

Delgaun's eyes dropped to the hem of the blue robe, and after a time he said :

" For Fergus it is over. You saw ? "

" Maur and I saw."

He lifted his head. " Where is Maur ? "

" He is gone. Look ! "

Maur was slowly moving away across the plain, a small and lonely speck in all that vastness.

"I sent him away," Alor replied to the wonder in Delgaun's eyes.

"He went?"

"He will do anything I tell him—for a little while." She smiled wisely, wistfully. "He is the second man I cannot hold. He is the songmaker."

"I was a songmaker, too."

"You keep your songs in your head. Maur will make his song about me, and he will be very unhappy, but he will be so proud of his song that he will have to think hard and then harder to nourish his unhappiness."

"The truth is with you, Alor, and you face it. Face it now!" His eyes met hers. "You know who I am?"

"I knew when you took the sword."

"I saw a woman die, and she was not wicked. You are not wicked. Death, only, moves where I move."

"That is not true."

"It is so. You must not move where I move. There is death."

"I will not move with you." Her voice was very quiet and gentle and strong.

"Where will you move then—if not with Maur?"

"That does not matter now. I am here to tell you what you will do. I know. That old unrest is dead for ever. It came to life briefly for a great need—for a great deed—to do a great justice—to atone a great evil. It is dead now for ever."

She stepped close to him, and he dropped his head before her, and brought his hands up to his breast. She put his own staff between his hands, and his hands came about the iron horn of it as of long habit.

"I will take the sword," said Alor.

He stood moveless while she unlooped the sword from his shoulders. She stood it between them, her hands on the cross of the hilt, and her voice, so sad and stirring, moved in his being.

"I too will be wise a little while—for your sake. Listen now! You will go southwards over the mountains to your father's house above the Rem, to hear the sea-birds' cry and see the gold bar of the sea under the setting sun. You will drink your father's wine and talk with men at the day's end, and peace will come about you there. And at the end of all you will sleep—and sleep—and sleep, and that will be best of all. That is what you will do, Delgaun."

"That is the thing I said to you." Delgaun spoke in his old deep voice. "Where is your peace?"

" I will find it. I know now—here in my heart—
that in the end I shall find peace."

" In the end we all find peace. It may be at that
end, only, will you find that peace."

" Let it be so."

She looked down, hiding her eyes, and her voice
reached him as if from a great distance.

" Peace only ! All my other seeking has been
finished this day."

Delgaun looked at that bent red womanly head.
He was his own man again, wise, reasoning, con-
siderate ; but there was a new strong man there too.
His voice was quiet still, and kindly, but it had
strength and assurance for two.

" I told you where to find peace, Alor, and it
stirred you. That place is still there. In that place
peace awaits you. You need have no fear."

Alor looked up then, and her eyes were dark and
deep.

" Peace is in your hands, Delgaun, and I have
no fear. I will go with you to that place."

" Let it be so," said Delgaun.


END OF PART ONE.

# PART TWO.

## FLANN OF THE LEFT HAND.

## CHAPTER XI.

### *The Man Who Was Sent.*

IT was on a fine evening of late Spring that Flann of the left hand, son of Orugh the swordmaker, and half-brother to Delgaun and Maur, came at last through the flanks of the mountains and saw again the sea.

The land, sloping away from his feet in sweeps of brown heather, cupped down into a wide and pleasant valley where a stream ran and glistered between cattle-dotted green pastures ; and at the foot of the valley was the gleam of a sea-fiord. The gleam and the green and the purple of it under the westering sun stirred Flann's heart, for it called to his mind his own Baravais and the bar of the sea beyond the point of Rem. Long Baravais ! that he would never see again, except in dreams.

At the head of the sea-fiord, where the stream spread to embrace the tide, there was a long curve of yellow strand, and, on this, many long-ships, eagle-prowed, were drawn up in line above high-water mark. Fighting ships—for the sun was

95

changing red and gold on the studded shields along the gunwales.

But the valley was all peace under the evening sun. Two long arrow flights back from the beach, and just above tidal water, a grey circular stone dun stood with its roots in the stream; and about it, on both banks, squatted a wide cluster of bothies roofed with the pale brown thatch of sea-bent. Blue smoke drifted lazily from black roof-vents; children and hounds moved and tumbled about open doors, and nowhere was there a gleam of any weapon. Along the slopes herd boys ho-ho-hoed black and dun cattle away from the narrow carse where young corn was already springing; and, near at hand, four women leant their breasts over a long yoke, and, behind them, a wooden plough shouldered aside the peaty black soil. An old man wrestled the single handle of the plough; his cracked voice intoned six notes of a tune to which the women's slow-driving feet kept time; and then the women added four notes to the six, threw up their braided black heads, and drove their shoulders against the yoke, making the old man stumble and curse. And the women laughed shrill as black-backed gulls, and again the old man took up the six slow notes of his song.

Flann stood long on the lip of the slope, his eyes carelessly roving, and then he strode down the deep-bitten track between tussocks of old heather, and so round the shoulder of a rock that stood ten feet out of the ground and leaned over as if to look into that pleasant valley.

"A place of work and laughter!" Flann mused aloud after the fashion of lonely men. "And of fighting men, too—poor fools! Why am I here?" The sardonic note was in his voice, and the sardonic line deepened from nostril to mouth corner. "What urge was on me? Did I not know that one place is the same and the very same as another place, and I only carrying my burden from one place to the same place?"

"Words to my very thought, man-with-one-hand!" said a strong, deep, quiet voice that might have been the voice of the rock that leaned and looked.

Flann's feet pivoted, knees bent, and his long staff of ash was thrust left-handed into the ground so that the forked iron head of it guarded his own. That iron-horned staff of ash had been round the world with Delgaun, his great brother.

A man leaned straight-shouldered against the rock, his bare fore-arms folded mightily below his breast. He was no common man. He was tall, rugged, dark, built to do and to endure. The strong bitten lines of his face showed that he was in his resolute, hard-come-by middle years, but there was one line there that had never come by taking thought. That was a terrible healed gash that had broken his left cheek-bone and left one eye sightless. The other eye had lost nothing of its power. That eye was deep-set, black, bold, stern, proud, watchful, thoughtful, kindly and wise. He wore a knee-length white tunic selvedged with blue and held at the waist by a bronze studded belt carrying the bronze leaf of a knife; and round his brow, holding his black hair, was a band of yellow gold with a polished agate dull-gleaming in it from the middle of his forehead. He was no common man.

The man, Flann, that that single bold eye considered was tall, too, but not too tall; wiry, tough, lean-legged below his brown cloak and saffron tunic; with cropped darkly fair hair above a long face, a mouth lined bitterly, and smoky blue eyes full of weariness. Eyes strangely weary and entirely unafraid. A man who had gone beyond all fear but the fear of his own thoughts. He held his ashen staff left-handed, and for a right hand he had a polished hook of red bronze.

The two men considered each other, not smiling, and then he of the one eye spoke, as if to himself, in his slow deep voice.

" Strange that his thoughts should run with mine."

" A way that thoughts have—when they run." Flann's mouth quirked.

" What man are you whose thoughts run—and run with mine ? "

" I am no more than Flann, son of Orugh who makes swords."

" I have heard of Orugh. He makes fine swords of iron in Long Baravais south of the Four Seas."

" Did you hear that one of his own swords killed two of his own sons ? "

" A way swords have when they are drawn. Will you tell me, Flann, son of Orugh, why you did not stay safe at home and you knowing that you only carry the same burden from one place to the same place ? "

" I would tell you that, man-with-the-one-eye," said Flann, " if you had the right to ask."

The other smiled and drew one finger down the gash in his cheek.

" I will not stand on my right," said he, " but in this place no one would care to deny me an answer."

" Then I know you ! You are Ingcel, son of the King."

" Son of the King if you like, but first I am Ingcel, Prince of Cumbria, in his own right."

" That name is in the mouths of men," said Flann. He was entirely unafraid. He tapped his staff with the bronze hook. " Must I answer your question, prince-in-his-own-right ? "

Ingcel the Prince answered that question in his own way.

"I came up here to this rock that is called The Watcher to reason with myself, and I cannot do it."

"I never heard of a man that could."

"And you came striding by, words in your mouth, and they were the words in my mind. For I, too, am urged to leave this valley that I shaped into peace between my hands, and I do not want to go."

"The thing that drove me would never drive a prince," said Flann ironically.

"Between us we could find out."

Flann's twisted mouth mocked himself and Ingcel and the world.

"If you want to know, Prince of Cumbria, I left my home in Baravais because I could no longer bear the sight of a woman, Alor, giving the breast to her son."

"And your son?"

"Not my son—nor my woman. But you are a prince and no woman dare drive you."

"Driven or drawn, you are wrong, I know." His finger smoothed his gashed cheek, and his one eye sought the ground musingly. "There is a woman at the heart of this—and a son, too—and I think that you were sent."

"A long road I was sent and I not knowing it."

" Nevertheless, you are here and I am here, and you came putting words to my thoughts. A man coming with one hand and without a sword. I should take that for an omen." He looked at Flann and smiled his slow smile. " Man-with-one-hand, were you sent to make up my mind for me ? "

" A man is always ready to make up another man's mind for him, if not his own."

" Try thou ! " Ingcel pointed a long black-haired arm down the valley. " See ! they come now. I told them come when the sun was at the loch's mouth."

Flann looked and saw a small company of men coming up the valley from the stone dun. A woman in a blue robe walked behind.

" They come, thinking their own thoughts, and their thoughts are not mine," said Ingcel. " That man in the red cloak, walking in front, is my father, Conmac the King. I am his eldest son, and he hates me to the marrow of my bones."

" He will have his own reason ? "

" He knows that I can be King at the lift of a finger."

" He would urge you to the world's end ? "

" And the dark gulf beyond it. But his urging is only the sound of a thin wind in my ears. Behind him are his eight sons, my brothers, and each has his own hope."

" They urge you, too ? "

"All but Eiccel, the youngest, who loves me.
And I could love them all. Look now, again!
That short wide man in the cloak of the beech
marten is Tulchinne the Pict, and he is here for
seven days, with envoys and long-ships, to offer me
the Kingship of Strathclyde."

"So that is your urge? A strong urge and a
strong kingdom!"

"But this is the heart of Cumbria. I made it,
and it is in my heart. Look at it!" He flung his
arm wide and pride was in his voice. "Look at it!
Men go about weaponless with no need to look over
shoulder; children herd the cattle that are safe from
all reivers; women sing at their work and make play
with an old man. I made that peace, and it cost
me one eye." He touched his broken cheek.
"Cuchulain the Hound gave me that, but he could
not break my grip. It was the price I paid, and the
urging of the Pictman is but the sound of water in
a place of stones. I am Ingcel of Cumbria."

"Life has no more to offer you?"

Ingcel came down from the high places of the
mind, and his dark face darkened.

"There you touch me, as you were meant to
touch me," he said in a low tone. "Life! It is
no miser, but it holds from me the one great thing.
I have no son."

He was silent then, looking over the heads of

the men coming up the slope. Flann looked, too, and he said :

" A woman walks there ? "

" Etir, my wife, daughter of the dead King of the Picts."

" She urges you, too ? "

" She does not urge me at all. She looks at me out of the quiet of her eyes and says nothing."

" And says nothing ! She is homesick for the Clyde ? "

" It could be." Ingcel moved his head slowly. " It could be so always. It is the way of the Picts. It is in her mind—it is in my own mind—that she would bear me a son by the waters of the Clyde. Now you know."

" I know." Flann lifted up his voice. " Ingcel of Cumbria, King of the Picts."

" Is that your word ? "

" It is what you know. There may be no son for you by Clyde waters, but in this place there will no longer be peace for you, straining against your wife's silence and desire—and against your own desire. And yet, unhappiness does not matter. It does not matter at all. You hunt and eat and sleep. You dream, you desire, you grasp. You think and talk and act. And the sun rises and the sun sets, and the old weary round goes on. And in the end you die, and death does not matter either. There is my word, King."

" Life has used you hard, Flann-with-one-hand."

" Life has not used me at all. That is my trouble. No ! My word is not finished. Life has shown me one small thing that is worth a little. One should keep one's trouble to oneself, and take his trouble away from those it would trouble."

" And so you are here where our roads meet, and bitter wisdom in your mouth."

" Cry Wisdom to-day, hail Death to-morrow ! "

Ingcel considered the lined mouth, the weary eyes that had no fear in them.

" You were sent," said he quietly, " and for two reasons."

" Again I go," said Flann, and lifted the point of his staff out of the heather. He took two long strides off the path so as to circle the approaching company. Ingcel's voice halted him.

" Stay, Flann, son of Orugh, and hear if I have heeded you ! "

" Where the roads cross pass quickly," said Flann, and took another long stride.

" Here, behind my shoulder, one-hand ! " ordered Ingcel sternly.

" The command of the King ! " said Flann, and turned back.

" King or Prince," said Ingcel, " I, too, am a man sent. I do not know why, but in my hands I will hold you."

There was only one man amongst the ten men that came worth looking at twice. That was Conmac, the King of North Britain. He was a small man and old in years, but no man might tell his age. His shoulders were curved, and his hair and beard and brows whiter than lint, but there was no line on his forehead, and his smooth cheeks were fresh as a maiden's. He had the patting, easy light gait of a trotting hound. His eyes were the colour of ripe sloes, hiding depth, hiding feeling, and as restless as the eyes of a bird. Flann, resting his bronze hook against the rock behind Ingcel, looked at him and felt a chill in his blood.

"Here is one," was his thought, "who, all his days, has done the good thing and the bad thing lightly as a fox, cunning as a weasel."

His eight sons behind him, tall and soldierly enough, were something less than mere men in his presence. Where he was they did not count. Flann's eyes went over them, and rested for a space on Eiccel, the youngest. He was still a stripling, and his mobile face and fair hair reminded Flann of his brother Maur, the song-maker.

Tulchinne, the regent of the Picts, was a squat man with a great spread of shoulder under his marten cloak. He had a sallow, sombre face above blue-black beard, nose all nostril, and eyes black and a little aslant.

The group of men faced Ingcel, moved restlessly, and were still. Eyes, slow to meet the single steadfast one, went to Flann where he leaned his bronze hook against the rock, his long face set in irony.

"Flann, the son of Orugh who makes iron swords," said the deep voice of Ingcel. "Our roads meet and move together for a while."

"To the same end, and it silent, O Ingcel," whispered Flann.

The old King took no notice of Flann. He came to the point at once, and his voice had the false high note of a eunuch's.

"There is an answer for us, my son?"

"There is an answer," said Ingcel quietly.

"We listen," said Conmac.

But before the answer could be given, the youngest brother, Eiccel, whose hands were clenched, cried out in his clear boy's voice:

"Take heed, Ingcel! Take care how you answer, brother of my heart."

He came impulsively through the heather, caught Ingcel at the hips, and shook at him. And Ingcel brought his hands down on the boy's wrists and held them.

"They plot against you, Ingcel," cried the youth. "There will be no peace in Cumbria when you are gone."

"Patience, little fool! If there be no peace in

Cumbria, let Britain look to a peace that will be desolate."

With the ease of his strength he unloosed the boy's grip and thrust him away. Eiccel whirled round on his father.

"You are my father," he cried desperately, "but you will spill my blood for this."

"The flat of my hand on your buttock, baby," said the King, and grinned wickedly.

Eiccel looked wildly about him, teeth and hands grinding, and then crying out, "I will not listen—I will not stay in this place," he flung away through the heather towards the upland moors.

But Ingcel was not to give his answer yet. Two of his brothers were pushed aside, and the woman, Etir, came between, her eyes only for her man, Ingcel. Straight and slowly she came to him, placed her hands on his shoulders, and drew herself up against him. The open blue sleeves, fringed with silver tassels, fell away and showed her long white arms. Tall and slender, a silver girdle on her hips, a silver fillet holding her black hair, her face as finely white as a white rose petal, her eyes as blue as deep water, that was Etir.

"Here in Cumbria we will stay, Ingcel man," she said softly. "We are happy here."

And Conmac, that wicked old one, furiously rubbed one finger across his white hound's teeth.

Ingcel did not look down into his wife's eyes.

He looked over her head at the far gleam of the sea, and his hands were clenched at his side.

"You were wrong, Flann one-hand," he murmured remotely, and Flann answered remotely, too:

"Silence yesterday, speech to-day—and in each the same meaning."

"It is not so," she whispered. "It is not so." She strained against Ingcel, and he was still as a rock. "Alas, Ingcel! Never, never could I change your mind."

"Etir is my mind now."

She said no other word. She touched his broken cheek softly, turned from him, and went slowly down the track to that valley in which happiness had lain.

Conmac cleared his throat, but Ingcel stopped his speech with open thrust hand and turned to Tulchinne the Pict.

"You are a great fighter, Tulchinne, and you are regent of the Picts as well. You hoped to be King?"

Tulchinne's face grew more sombre, but he did not answer at once. Then he said:

"There are too many Tulchinnes on the Clyde for one to be King—this time."

"Hold that in your mind—it is your due. Here is my answer: I will go with you to the Clyde, and if the people want me I will be King."

"The people want you," said Tulchinne surlily. "It is my message."

And Conmac on his own hidden track said:

"When do you go, Ingcel, my son?"

But Ingcel did not heed him.

"Listen ye now!" he said, his voice cold and stern. "I am going from this place but my arm is long, and young Eiccel will be my other eye in Cumbria. Any man, King or prince or robber, who hurts the peace that I made will answer to me at the world's end. That is all." He looked at Conmac, and his mouth-corner twitched. "I speak to you now, my father. It is the custom to take presents where one goes royally, and I will take to Clydach what is due, but not from Cumbria."

Conmac shifted on his feet and his voice was higher than ever.

"Nine sons, and they all hungry——"

"Then you would give with a grudge. Let it be! I will take nothing from Britain now, but if I am driven to it I will take so much and spill so much that the grandson's grandson will remember." He turned to Tulchinne, the glowering Pict. "You heard me, Tulchinne?"

"I heard you, King," growled Tulchinne. "Gifts will be expected."

"And will be given, but not by toll on Cumbria. I will put my Pictmen to the test. Listen! You have six long ships fully manned. To-morrow one of them will take water for the Clyde with my wife Etir and her women. To your five I will match five of mine, and we will show Erin that the Picts have a new King."

"For that game I am always ready," said Tulchinne, a new gleam in his eye.

"There is a young King in Tara called Conaire of the Birds, a man of peace, and there is word that his young soldiers, in leash at home, are for reiving overseas. We will strike first, and at Tara, and make the Clyde gunwale deep.

"Whatever you say, O Ingcel," agreed Tulchinne.

"Ye can go now," said Ingcel shortly. He turned to Flann. "That is the road you are going, Flann Left-hand, the sea road to Erin, famous for its wealth and its lore and its secret rites."

"One road is the same as another," said Flann wearily, "even if it ends in the hollow of a wave."

# CHAPTER XII.

## *The Sea Road.*

IT was on the morning of the third day, somewhere south of the Calf of Falga, with the beacon torches still smoking on the prows of the long-ships, that Ingcel put the side-hole of the curved, yard-long war-horn to his lips and sent its auroch bellow across the waters.

The sea that had been empty full circle about them for two days was empty no longer. From the head of a great surge the prowman had sighted a black lugsail, and, as he cried and pointed, another sail and another lifted out of the valleys of the sea behind the leading boat.

The breeze, light and pleasant, was dead out of the west; the sail of Ingcel's boat was furled at the foot of the short mast, and eight pairs of oars swung and checked and bit in a slow rhythm. But though the breeze was light the running sea was tremendous—not a dangerous sea, but a colossal one. Somewhere, on the waste of waters south of Erin, a hurricane had stirred the depths of ocean and set it moving a thousand miles. These were not waves, but curving easy hills of water without foam.

In the hollows there was a murmurous quiet in a deep wide valley all green and grey and purple, and head had to be thrown back into shoulders to look up at the crown of the slope tipped with translucent green where the young sun shone through. When the high prow struck the slope the water whispered along the gunwale before the boat lifted for the long crawl to the broad head of the hill in full sunlight, with the immense heave of the sea all about shining gold and silver and grey green. And looking back and down one saw the other boats of the fleet strung out from crown to crown, and looking forward one saw a black sail lifting and a black sail sinking.

Again the war-horn roared from Ingcel's boat, and the oars of the other boats swung to a new rhythm. They were closing in on their leader to take up battle order ; and in a little while the fleet was moving forward slowly in a narrow wedge. So great were the hills of water that the fighting wedge was spaced between the crowns of two waves.

Ingcel fitted his winged helmet over his black brows, stepped up on the steering platform, and took the broad-bladed rudder oar from the steersman. Flann sat on the edge of the platform, his brown cloak loose on his shoulders, and his long chin resting on his hand over the iron horn of his staff; and there was a faint, pitying, aloof smile about his closed mouth. Twelve fighting men were in station along the gunwales behind the high prow, shields on arms, throwing spear in hand; and a bundle of throwing spears laid ready across the thwarts. Behind them and guarded by them, the eight pairs of rowers swung slowly and yet more slowly.

Soon it was clear that the oncoming fleet was not a large one, but large enough. At no time more than three or four sails could be seen at once, but a seaman's eye might gather that there was a total of not more than twelve long-ships, all of the wide-beamed model built in Erin, prowed with the carved head of strange birds, and with round bossed shields gleaming along the gunwales. The western breeze was light and they came slowly, the foam curling on their blunt bows, the tall prows thrown high on the summit of a great wave and tipping down slow and stately.

The oncoming fleet went into battle order less than a quarter mile away. The black sails came down, the bronze shields went inboard, the oars swung out, and wedge was pointed against wedge.

Flann looked up at Ingcel, tall above him on the steering platform, one hand easy on the rudder oar. His dark face was set, carved like oak, his gashed cheek like knotted wood, his one eye intent on the sea in front of him.

"The road to kingship might end in the hollow of a wave," murmured Flann. "I said that."

"I heard you." Ingcel's face did not change. "A man or two in Erin had a thought like my own. But we are not fighting yet. Be silent and watch!"

From the crests of two hills, the sea whispering all round them, the leading boats looked at each other across the empty, soughing hollow. And there Ingcel lifted up his left hand, fingers spread, and three times waved it crosswise above his head. There was a pause, and then the man at the rudder oar of the other boat copied Ingcel's gesture.

"We will parley," said Ingcel, and gave an order to the man at the leading oar.

The two boats were on one billow now, and they slanted prows away from each other as they came nearer; but the oars were nearly touching as they came side by side in the hollow of the sea. Then the oars checked, the water gurgling over the blades, and the fighting men looked aside at each other with appraising eyes. The other boats kept station behind the leaders, and the great seas swung under them; and sometimes, except for the two boats side-by-side on the crest of a wave, one fleet was hidden from the other.

Ingcel stood at ease against the lift of the sea,

his thigh against the rudder oar ; Flann sat sideways at his knees, swaying with the sway, his staff under his chin, his eyes alive, but still weary.

"That young cock will fight at a word," was the thought in his mind as he looked at the steersman of the Irish boat.

He was young, tall, supple, with flashing dare-devil eyes, and a mane of yellow hair below a round helmet. On the platform with him stood two other young men as like him as peas in the same pod, and leaning on the platform was another youth with a bare head of tossing flax-fine hair about a strangely livid face, and eyes, nearly pale as his hair, surface-gleaming with a strange light. On the side thwart, side-by-side, sat three red men, with hard-bitten faces above the rims of their red shields. There was not an old man in the whole crew. Young hawks on their first foreign harry, and dangerous as fire.

"Ingcel must be wise now," said Flann to himself.

And Ingcel was no fool. He spoke first.

"I am Ingcel of Cumbria on a voyage to Alba."

"I have heard of Ingcel one-eye," said the steersman, "and hoped to meet him—but not so soon." He laughed a little mockingly. "Is it Ingcel's geasa that makes him take the long road to Alba righthandwise round Falga?"

"I have no geasa," said Ingcel evenly. "But

it was in my mind to visit Conaire of Tara who has nine.''

'' And Conaire the High King would make you welcome—after his fashion.''

The youth with the toss of flaxen hair and mad eyes leant over to look into Ingcel's boat.

'' See all the kingly presents he has for Conaire the High King! Shields on arm and spears pointed,'' he cried, and showed all his teeth.

'' The High King might give us a present or two to take to Alba,'' said Ingcel, still smoothly.

'' Gold and silver and bronze, kine and swine and stallions—and other presents for one seeking them over the hilt,'' hinted the steersman.

'' You know Conaire, I think? ''

'' I am Fer Rogain, his foster-brother,'' said the lad proudly. '' These are my brothers, Fer Gair and Fer Le, and he that laughs is my brother, Lomna Druth.''

'' I have heard of Conaire and his foster-brothers,'' said Ingcel. '' Has he tired of them at last? ''

All the world had heard of Conaire and his nine geasas. Geasa means a restriction or tabu. He was called Conaire the Great, and he was that. He was the first King within the Four Seas to rule without the sword. A beardless youth when he took his seat on the Lia Fail—the Stone of Destiny, the coronation stone that is now said to be under

Edward's chair at Westminster—he set his heel on rapine and on wanton killing, and held the peace of Erin in his two young strong hands for half a score of years.

His genealogists—every King had three or four—called him Conaire the son of Eterscel, but a woman here and there might whisper to another woman a scandalous story that his real father was Nemglan, King of the Birds, that is, King of that tribe whose totem was a bird—a white bird of the sea brown-speckled, which is a solan goose in its first season. Whether or no, it is certain that one of his geasas, or restrictions, was that he must not kill any bird. That one geasa he never broke. He had eight others, handed down to him, in the tradition of his tribe, generation after generation ; and that is why he was sometimes called Conaire of the Birds and sometimes Conaire of the Nine Geasas. Here are the nine :

    *I. Thou shalt not cast at or slay birds;*

    *II. Thou shalt not come righthandwise round*
          *Tara and lefthandwise round Bregia;*

    *III. Thou shalt not hunt the two evil wolves of*
          *Cerna;*

    *IV. Thou shalt not go out for more than nine*
          *nights from Tara;*

    *V. Thou shalt not sleep in a house in which*
          *light is manifest after sunset;*

> VI. *Three Reds shall not fare before thee to the House of Red;*
>
> VII. *No rapine shall be wrought in thy kingship;*
>
> VIII. *After sunset a company of one woman and one man shall not enter the house in which thou art; and*
>
> IX. *Thou shalt not heal the quarrel between two of thy septs.*

It could be that, one time or another, one or other of these nine might be a wise enough tabu for this man or that, but the growing foolish total of them on one man's shoulders was a burden not easily borne. Conaire, while minding the old rule that one should not make a custom or break a custom, was careless of them all, except one. That one was the seventh, forbidding him and others the wicked pleasures of Rapine. That geasa tuned with his own character, and he kept it with all his might. For years of plenty there was no rapine wrought in his royal dominion of Meath. And then four men that he loved and that loved him broke that one precious geasa.

They were his foster-brothers: Fer Rogain, Fer Gair, Fer Le, and Lomna Druth, the sons of Donn Desa, army-captain of Tara. Fer Rogain was the leading spirit and had iron in him; Fer Gair and Fer Le were merely his smudged copies; Lomna

Druth copied no one. Lomna Druth was mad and had the second sight.

The five youths—the King and his four foster-brothers—used wear the same bright raiment and the same shining bronze armour, ride horses that were matched in colour and pace, dip fingers in the one dish, think the same thoughts about love and wine and song-making—but not about war. The great peace that lay on Tara like a blanket itched the four sons of Donn Desa, who was the son and the grandson and the great-grandson of soldiers and army champions; and the recognised way of champions was to take the thing they wanted and slay the man that protested. They had, in truth, a prescribed right to the three Bad Gifts: the Gift of Robbery, the Gift of Slaughter, and the Gift of Rapine. And Conaire had deprived them of the gifts as a king will—without a by-your-leave.

The four brothers squirmed and whispered, and wondered what their kingly foster-brother would do if they reived as much as one small swine. And the very wonder finally set their feet on the red road in a sheer gay dare-deviltry. They lifted a boar here, an ox there, a milking cow yonder, trounced a land-owner that threatened them with the king, and kissed his woman to drive the lesson home.

Conaire said nothing and did nothing, for he did not care to curb his brothers on too tight a rein. There was a glut of swine and kine in Erin; the flat of a sword would hardly raise a weal on the tough hide of a farmer; there was never yet a woman the worse for a little kissing; and no blood had been shed and no woman stolen.

The lads, as lads will, grew bolder as they grew older. They gathered round them a company of half-fledged young devils, the sons of under-kings and chiefs and soldiers, rapscallions like the seven Manes of Connacht, the sons of Maeve; the three red-hound brothers of Cualla named Clotach, and Cetach, and Conal; Crinach Farsuin of Ulster; many others; in all a company of four hundred unwhipped wolf-cubs more dangerous than any four-footed beast in the woods of Cerna. Soon, then, they were reiving in the full measure, and enjoying the three bad gifts. Strong houses were raided, spoils shared, blood spilled, women stolen and hidden. And promptly Conaire put the weight of his hand on them in kingly fashion. He swung wide a net of veterans under MacEcht, his champion, gathered in as many of the leaders as were caught in the mesh, brought them hand-tied to Tara, and called their fathers and grandfathers to his council hall. The fathers and grandfathers came in a hurry, and a mother or two ready for weeping.

"It was my geasa that rapine be not wrought in my reign," said Conaire mildly. "Ye knew that?"

"Your foster-brothers knew it, too," said proud Maeve, who was there with tame Aillil and tamed Fergus.

"No better than your seven Manes," said the King, mildly still. "My geasa, the geasa of the tribe I swear by, is broken, and it is my right to command each father to slay his son, or his seven sons."

"And your foster-brothers?"

"I can do what I like with my foster-brothers," said the King in his high-kingly way.

"Right, O Right!" cried old Donn Desa. "The slaying shall be done for thee, Conaire beloved. I await your word." And he placed one hand on his sword and the other on Fer Rogain's neck.

Conaire looked them over, his eyes cold and blue, and many a father flinched, and the mothers brought the first peal of the lament for the dead to the roots of the tongue. But after a while Conaire shook his head.

"Blood has been spilled in wantonness," said he sadly, "but spilling blood now will not fill any slack vein."

"Hang the young whelps and no blood will be spilled," advised black MacEcht, the King's champion.

"Do not let me be as big a fool as yourself, my poor MacEcht," said the King irritably, and let his eye rest on Fer Rogain. Fer Rogain did not flinch, and he held his mouth from smiling.

" I am looking at you, Fer Rogain, and you thinking how pithless I am because of the love I bear you. It is true that I will not kill, but I will do worse. Before this game is played you will be sorry that you did not hang. You wanted your three gifts and you shall have them, for I will send you to that place where there are masters in the game. Listen you ! " His voice was cold as wind. " You are banished from Erin for one year and one day—you and the men you led. I have twelve long-ships waiting you at Inver Colpa, and a veteran or two to advise you. Let you raid Britain where Conmac the King is old and strong and venomous. Let you raid Ingcel of Cumbria, remembering how he made Cuchulain turn tail and hanged three score reivers of the Red Branch. Let you, indeed, visit Ingcel, and if you escape him, let you raid Alba, where the Picts have a secret way of sacrificing prisoners on tables of stone in the heart of an oak wood. A year and a day ! And what is left of ye will come to me here at Tara, and if I am kind I will kill ye then, so that ye no more dream of terror and pain past bearing. Go now ! "

And they went. But they were not in the least unhappy or fearful. They told each other that they had the luck of the world, and that their

darling Conaire was no more than hiding his gifts
behind the rasp of a rough tongue. Twelve long-
ships and four hundred fighting men! What more
could young smiters need to face all the world?
Britain and Cumbria and Clydach, and even
Dalriada itself, where terrible men of their own
blood lived. They took to the oars singing, and
went out on the shoulders of the sea; and the
fortunate west wind came up behind them, and the
black sails filled.

And here, now, on the wide wastes of sea, Fate
had drawn the raiding fleets prow to prow, and Fer
Rogain was playing a game of life and death with
Ingcel.

"I have heard of Conaire and his foster-
brothers," said Ingcel. "Has he tired of them at
last?"

"I would not go as far as that with you," said
Fer Rogain. "But, all the same, he sent us to
visit Ingcel in Cumbria."

"And Ingcel has his own way of giving
presents."

"And now the time," cried Fer Rogain,
grimly gay.

"Time enough," said Ingcel easily, "the day
before us."

"As you say, but we must make a beginning
some time."

"This wolf has a tongue," said Flann to himself.

Ingcel looked down the slope of the sea, fingering the gash of his cheek, and Flann knew that his mind was working in ice.

"I see that you have twelve ships to my ten," said he. "Will you hold by the fair play of fighting men?"

"What else? Ship to ship and no more."

"And has it come into your mind that we might not fight at all?"

The middle man of the three red men laughed. Clotach his name.

"That is not Ingcel, the man who fought Cuchulain?"

"I have fought so many, red man," said Ingcel, "that I am no longer afraid not to fight. I will fight if I must, but, as we all know, when the fight is done if there are not four ships on the shoulders of the sea there will be less. Cumbria you will never see."

"Nor you Tara."

"And there is an end. But, mark this, besides Cumbria there are Cymri, and Mercia with the breed of Cuchulain, and Ormlyth, and all North Britain. And besides Tara there are Ulster and Uriel and Bregia and all Leinster."

Fer Rogain frowned, his eyes watchful.

"What is in your mind, Ingcel?"

" I am an older man than you and I can say what is in my mind. It is this. We are on the sea for spoil. Instead of slaughter without spoil let us join fleets."

" And then ? "

" Then for a raid on Erin I will give you a raid on Britain."

" And where would the first destruction fall ? "

" By cast of lot, thumb-breadths on your sword."

" Do not heed him," cried Lomna Druth, his hair lifting and his eyes mad. " There is a doom in it. In my bones I know it ! Who would trust a dark man with one eye ? "

Ingcel kept that one eye steadily on Fer Rogain, and his voice was steady, too.

" Ingcel keeps his pledges. It is known. If you agree, I and two with me will go into your ship, and you and two of your brothers will come into mine."

Fer Rogain considered this, his fingers plucking at a gold torque on his breast, and before he spoke the blood came up to his face as if in a half-shame.

" There are two veterans and the seven Manes in the ship behind me," he said. " I would talk to them."

" And I will talk to Tulchinne the Pict." Ingcel gestured a hand and the oars backed water. And as the boats moved apart he lifted up his voice.

"I am done parleying, Fer Rogain. If fight it is, raise your hand with your sword in it."

Flann found his heart beating high in his breast. "There is fear in me still, and I know it," he whispered to himself. "Life and the love of it is knotted in my bones, and the craven in me does not want to drown in the hollow of a wave." He looked up at Ingcel, steadying his voice.

"They will fight?"

"Not this time—unless the mad one taunt them to it. This Fer Rogain has a strong core and knows that I speak truth. Moreover, they are born reivers and a destruction is their delight."

"And you will give them one on your father's kingdom?"

"That is how I am a prince and a King," said Ingcel grimly. "My father and brothers are safe in Cumbria, and will stay there making friends with my people and plotting against Eiccel. But three days south of Cumbria is Ormlyth, and Gabur, its prince, is the man I fear. Five years ago I taught him a lesson, but he is apt to forget it now that a boy holds Cumbria. We might teach him a last lesson this time."

"It is evil to be a King," said Flann.

"Call me evil at the end of our road, one-hand."

"If I have a tongue," said Flann.

# CHAPTER XIII.

## *Gabur's Last Lesson.*

IT was night-time, supper over, and Gabur the
Red, Prince of Ormlyth, was pressing flagons on
Conmac his King, and on the seven sons of
Conmac, in the wide, low, oak-beamed hall of his
new wooden house at Ormlyth.

The women had gone to their own place, and the
great hall was crowded with men, most of them
rough, shag-headed warrior-men out of the hills.
Crusie lamps flamed murkily from the walls; the
long tables had been cleared of the broken meats;
dogs crunched bones in the rushes, snarling at each
other, yelping to indifferent kicks; bellied brown
jars of muddy mead were scattered on the board,
and men, dipping wooden methers therein, drank
and drank again, roared open-mouthed to each
other, sang rude songs. Two men wrestled
savagely in a corner, and a third man, swaying on
his heels, looked carelessly on over the rim of a
half-full piggin. The wrestler who was having the
worst of it tried to get a hand to a short iron knife

at his hip, but the onlooker plucked it from its sheath and threw it with a poor aim at a dog. Then the defeated man fell, and the victor, giving him a knee in the groin, left him squirming, and snatched the spattering piggin from the onlooker's mouth. And a new wrestle started with fury.

At the high table, near the open fireplace, where bog-pine blazed over white ashes, there were only Gabur, Conmac, and Conmac's seven sons. The eighth son, young Eiccel, sat at the fire-corner, his elbows on his knees and his hand chafing a wrist that showed a red welt where a cord had been bound too tightly. Ingcel had left Eiccel as his regent in Cumbria, but old Conmac had plans of his own, and here in Ormlyth was Eiccel, a sullen, frightened boy, with sullen, watchful eyes turned underbrows towards the table.

Conmac the White Fox had stayed only three days at Ingcel's dun, long enough to make sure that stress of weather would not force Ingcel to return. Then, in a forced march of three days, he had come south to Ormlyth, and here he was at Red Gabur's table with eight heads close about him to listen to his silky whispering. There was no need to whisper, but whispering suited the foul plot that was being hatched.

" Five hundreds will be enough and to spare," he was whispering. " Ingcel has taken the pick of the fighters, and the fat and lazy ones left have not faced the stress of war for five years."

"They faced it well that time," growled Gabur, his hand under his red hair where an ear was missing.

"There is no one to lead them now, you fool. Fat and lazy, I tell you, and fat and ripe the spoil; and if you do your work well Ingcel will never know that the raiders from the hills are out of Ormlyth."

Gabur turned a thumb towards the fire-corner.

"Your calf will take word to him."

"You will burn all the boats that are left."

"He will walk on his two feet."

"And tell Ingcel how he was brought to Ormlyth, his hands tied," added one of the brothers.

Conmac's flat thumb pressed hard on the table and his voice was irritable at last. "Ye are too stupid. I have thought of all that. Eiccel will tell nothing, it might well be."

"Let it be as you say, my father, but the thing can never be hidden from Ingcel."

Gabur swore savagely and thrust himself upright from his chair, his eyes staring down the length of the room.

"By my father's bones, Ingcel knows already!"

One of the valves of the double-door at the end

of the hall had opened quietly, and in the opening stood tall Ingcel himself, winged helmet on head, shield on arm, iron sword in hand ; and his fierce black eye looked at them over the heads of the revellers.

" I will take him now," said Gabur, clawing at his knife.

" Fool ! " Conmac gripped his arm. " Let us take him with a smooth tongue till his back is turned. Send word out to gather your men. He has only three hundred with him, and we have Cumbria under our hands for good and all."

But there the double-door burst wide open, and a press of fighting men drove Ingcel forward : tall, golden young men with shields of bronze ; broad, dark men with leather targes ; brown, strong men with swords of iron.

" Ingcel before me where I go," roared the boar Gabur, wresting his arm free and leaping.

The drunken crew had not yet time to know the thing that was on them, and they scattered aside from his drive down the hall.

" Here is for you, Ingcel one-eye ! " He crouched his head into his shoulders and leaped for Ingcel's throat.

But Ingcel stepped easily, almost lazily, aside from that blind leap, and his long iron blade came shearing downwards. Gabur was dead as he struck the ground, his last lesson learnt.

Then the press of fighting men burst by, and the clangour shook the black rafters.

Down at the beach, half a mile away, where the brown waters of the Rib estuary eddied by the muddy sand, the line of long-ships was drawn up, with half a hundred men on guard ; and a hundred paces inland, where the crisp sea-grass lipped high-water mark, Flann left-hand walked up and down, his pointed iron-horned staff pricking into the sod. The glow as of a mighty bonfire wavered around him and shone down the beach on the shields of the guard and the high prows of the ships. But Flann went on pacing, never lifting his head towards the fire and the clamour.

There, half a mile inland, the huddled bothies of the half town of Ormlyth were ablaze, and the biggest blaze of all lifted above the high roof of Gabur's wooden house. That blaze lit up the flat land down to the sea and made the grass a bright green. A clanging and shouting came down on the breeze, and above the shouting of men in savage joy or savage terror lifted the shrieking wail of women. But Flann only shrugged one shoulder and went on pacing.

" A mad world," said he, " and it will make an end of the mad ones—and of me before the road ends."

But a nearer shouting stayed his steps, and he turned to see a dark, slender figure running towards him across the grass. Behind, and not far behind, came another figure, bounding hugely, even merrily, and shouting—the gay, exultant shouting of the hunter with the game in full view and the bay at hand.

The hunted came straight for Flann, and Flann threw his staff on guard. And then he saw that the runner was Eiccel, the young brother of Ingcel, spent to the last gasp, his mouth open and his eyes wild. He circled round Flann, whirled, and caught him under the oxters as a shield.

"A weapon!" he panted. "A weapon! Let me die like a man."

The pursuer came in great bounds, and stopped dead, both heels into the ground. He was laughing wide-mouthed and showing his teeth to the gums. His flax hair stood up with life in it, and his eyes were yellow. He was Lomna Druth, the mad buffoon brother of Fer Rogain.

"Give him another run for it, one-hand," he shouted.

"No-no!" cried Flann, warding him off with his staff. "This is Ingcel's brother."

"Death—his brother—what do I mind! Five my lucky number, and fifth is he. Out of my way, cripple, and let him run!"

He dashed his shield against Flann's staff, and drove Flann aside; and Eiccel, staggering, leapt away from the bloody sword. Lomna Druth leapt after, but, in the middle of the leap, Flann's staff was thrust deftly between his legs, and he went down on his face with a clang. The iron horn of the staff clamped on his neck to pin him, but the madman, not heeding the pain, wrenched himself over on his side ; and Flann, choosing his spot carefully, kicked him in the split of the breast bone. Lomna Druth grunted and collapsed, and Flann set a foot on his twisting form. And Flann, though he was a man of peace and weary of life, felt a fine savage small glow warm in him.

Two other figures came running across the flat, but not pursuer and pursued. These two ran shoulder to shoulder. One was Ingcel, and the other that tall, blonde young devil, Fer Rogain.

Eiccel staggered forward, and Ingcel threw a strong arm about him.

"They bound me, brother," the lad gasped. "They brought me bound."

"Steady, little one, steady!" Ingcel clasped him firmly, his shield against his shoulders, but Eiccel had to speak the things in his mind.

"Be on your guard, Ingcel. They plot to raze your dun to the ground."

"To the ground they are razed, King of Britain," said Ingcel deeply.

Fer Rogain was facing Flann, the leaf of his bronze sword below shield, and Flann, staff on guard, kept his foot on Lomna Druth.

"You killed him, one-hand?"

"I did my best, but I feel life under my heel," and with that firm heel he drove Lomna Druth's breast against the ground. He was not afraid any more.

Ingcel, holding Eiccel, came between, and faced Fer Rogain.

"This is he, Eiccel, my brother," he said. "Flann saved his life—and your mad brother's life as well."

"A bad thing if we killed him on you," said Fer Rogain.

"Bad enough you have done on me," said Ingcel. "Ye have killed my father and seven of his sons."

Fer Rogain's mouth opened and shut. "Your father and seven sons?"

"Under that roof flaming. I saw that sword under your shield at the throat of Conmac, my father."

Fer Rogain fell back a pace, lowered his shield, and looked at the red-stained bronze sword. He looked at it a long time. Then he wiped it, this side and that, across his thigh, threw it up in the air and caught it by the tip. He placed the hilt in Ingcel's hand.

"It is your due. Strike here!"

He pulled the gold torque aside, and bared his breast for the blow. Ingcel placed the point against the white skin. The point bit, and one drop of blood trickled on the blade.

"Blood for blood, it is my due, blood brother." Ingcel, in turn, threw the sword in the air, caught the tip and placed the hilt in Fer Rogain's hand. And Fer Rogain's breath, that had been hard held for death, went out in a deep sigh.

Flann took his foot off Lomna Druth, and the mad one stumbled to his feet, a hand below his breast. His brother, Fer Rogain, struck him open-handed across the mouth.

"Mad one! You would kill a youth unarmed?"

The mad one did not heed the blow, though the blood stained his white teeth.

"My number is five," he shrilled, "and I hold one in my little finger." He turned to Flann wickedly. "You are that one, the fifth in my own time, left-hand." He laughed wildly, and the whites of his eyes gleamed in the wavering glow. "And after that I will die—die. I see my head fall between wide door posts and my body walking three steps headless."

He flung round on Ingcel, the flame of prophecy still in his mad eyes.

"You will wreak your destruction in Erin, Ingcel one-eye, and every eye in Erin shall weep."

## CHAPTER XIV.

### *The Web is Spun.*

THE blowing winds of the equinox had gone by, and the great swells had smoothed themselves out, when at last the fleets saw the hills and woods of Erin over the high prows. An evening with young summer in the balm of the breeze, and the wavelets rippling gold and green. Two stone-ribbed headlands made horns to a wide bay, and two conical peaks stood up in purple above the filmy young green of new-clad woods. Between headland and headland, behind flats of yellow sand, there was nothing but forest and more forest lifting inland south and west to the breast of rounded heather hills.

The long-ships were no longer strung out across the sea. Here, within sight of land, they moved close together and slowly, sails down, oar almost touching oar, prow over stern, so that no one looking from the shore might gather the strength of the fleet. Fer Rogain, tall on the steering platform of

Ingcel's boat, pointed a long arm and spoke across to Ingcel, pride in his voice :

"Erin for you now, land of honey and gold and green!"

It was Tulchinne the Pict that answered back.

"Honey and gold for us, and the green burned brown!"

Fer Rogain went on addressing Ingcel. "The Liffe River flows there between sand banks, and a league above the mouth is a village called Ath Cliath."

"Not a village that will pay us," said Tulchinne, "but a town with a prince's dun."

"You speak before your king," said Fer Rogain coldly.

"A bad habit I have." Tulchinne grinned unashamed.

"There will be a cure for it," said Ingcel quietly, his one eye over the green woods. "A land of gold and honey, but these can wait. Our first need is water and meat."

Fer Rogain nodded twice to show that the same thought was in his own mind.

"North of Ben Atair, that stone hill, my father, Donn Desa, has an island of sheep and spring water——"

"But your father?"

"He will not be there. Only three herdsmen."

" A blood sacrifice—even a herdsman's blood—is a good thing to start with," said the pagan Pict.

" We are not here to kill herds for sacrifice," Ingcel told him sternly. " Well, Fer Rogain ? "

" I offer you that island as my first gift, to show faith. We must land under the night, for there is a beacon against raiders, and that is why I brought you here with Ben Atair to hide us."

" Many a notable raid will you lead," praised Ingcel.

" We can land on a strand I know, kill the sheep we want ; and after that I will tell you what is in my mind. If you are pleased we can make a plan."

" We will do that," agreed Ingcel.

And so, under the cover of a night lit thinly by a moon in its first quarter that made the sea a wan and bleak silver and the oar surge whiter than snow, the fleet came quietly to shore on a narrow strand on the landward side of that island that is now called Lambay.

The plans were already made. As soon as the keels grated, Fer Rogain with ten men slipped into the thigh-deep water, waded ashore, and ran inland. The herders' bothy was in a hollow over the first rise, and, as Fer Rogain and his men poured down the slope, two half-wolf dogs rushed forward barking, and fled yowling. The rug-headed fore-herd, half awake, stumbled out of the doorway as Fer Rogain reached it, and Fer Rogain caught him by collar and arm.

"You are not a dead man yet, Snecht," he said, bringing his face close.

The fore-herd swallowed his heart.

"Welcome, prince! You did not stay long in Britain?"

"Long enough to bring hungry friends to taste your mutton."

"To be sure. How many?"

"One or two, but they eat. Say half a hundred of your fat ones."

"Your father, Donn Desa, will not like this, little prince."

"You will like it less if he comes to know of it from your lit beacon. Rout your men out and gather us a flock, Snecht boy."

In less than an hour the faggots from the beacon on the hill-top were glowing in a score of cooking fires along the bottom of the shallow glen, and the reivers were busy cooking and eating and talking and laughing, and cooking and eating, and after that cooking and eating.

Around the mid-fire the leaders made a ring. Ingcel with Flann behind his shoulder, young Eiccel, the three sons of Donn Desa, mad Lomna Druth head down sucking a marrow bone, Tulchinne the Pict his marten cloak about his hips, the Manes of Maeve, the three red brothers of Cualla, Crinach Farsuin of Ulster, a few others.

Fer Rogain and young Eiccel sat side by side. Since that night at Ormlyth, when death had so nearly touched them, a tie of liking had knotted itself between the two, and now they sat shoulder to shoulder toasting ribs of lamb on pointed sticks, driblets of fat sizzling on the embers. Fer Rogain examined his rib judiciously, gave it a final toast, tasted it, and put it under Eiccel's nose.

" Your teeth in that, young one ! ''

Eiccel bit deep, chewed, swallowed, nodded with satisfaction, tasted his own rib, and passed it to Fer Rogain.

" Your own teeth in that, brother.''

And after a while Fer Rogain threw dead sticks on the fire so that it blazed up to gleam on men's eyes and bring out the strong lines of cheek and jaw. Then he spoke.

" Ingcel will not have heard of the Bruden of Da Derga ? ''

" I will hear of it, Fer Rogain,'' said Ingcel, wiping his fingers on a handful of old grass.

" It is a secret we keep to ourselves from the world. After the King's House at Tara, the Bruden of Da Derga is the noblest big house in Erin.''

" By the fingerbones of my father ! '' swore Clotach, one of the red men of Cualla. " No one would give that noble, generous hostel to the flame and the sword?''

''After what Ingcel has suffered at my hands,'' said Fer Rogain, ''there is only one house in Erin I would not offer to Ingcel for his destruction, and that is the house of Conaire the King.''

Lomna Druth shook his hair out of his mad eyes and cried:

''Maybe you are giving him the jewel you would guard.''

''Jewels and gold I will give him.''

''Tell us of this great house and we will judge for ourselves,'' growled Tulchinne the Pict.

''I will tell ye,'' said Fer Rogain in the leisurely voice of the story-teller. ''Da Derga the Red is a man who loves good company, kingly or in rags. Good company, rich feasting, songs and stories without end, feats of skill and strength, these are the things he likes, and he took his own way to bring them to his doors. He built a hostel where all men and the pick of women are his guests, where no man pays a toll, and where women pay how they like.''

''Or how I like,'' said Tulchinne the Pict.

''A strange thing,'' went on Fer Rogain, ''he did not build his hostel on any of the great chariot roads of Erin, nor on any road that goes from one place to another place. He built it on a road of his own, whereon if a man, prince or beggar, set

his foot, he does so to visit Da Derga and no one
other. Look! over there across the dark is the
Strand of Fuirbthe, and behind it is a waste of
sand hills, and beyond the sand, where the woods
begin, runs the road of Mid Luchair. South on
that road is the Liffe River and beyond that river
is the road of Cualla."

" My own darling road! " said Red Clotach.

" Two leagues south on that road there is a fork,
and one prong of it goes to Naas-na-Righ, the
palace of the King of Leinster, and the other prong
goes left-hand towards the hills ; a narrow road
and you might miss it and you not looking for it,
but, setting foot on it you would come to the end
and the last end of it at the doors of Da Derga's
Hostel.

" That Hostel is built at the mouth of a green
glen with oak trees and pasture in the hollows, and
furze yellow on the slopes, and heather on the round
crowns. And the Dothra River flows out of the
glen, and the Hostel is built across the water. A
great house! Strong oak the walls, rye reed on the
high roof, and all the door posts carved with strange
beasts and coloured yellow and red and green.
There are seven doorways in the full ring of the
wall, and seven passages, and seven rooms to each
passage ; and a centre-court under the sky, with
the Dothra River flowing across it and under the
walls. That is the hostel. But mark you! Though

there are seven doorways there is only one door, and that door is shut in the eye of the wind. The other six doorways are wide to the world day and night, from year's end to year's end. A man or a company will come in at any hour, and the door-wards will point the way and the nose lead the way to where the tables are spread and the cooking pots at the bubble. And that man or that company will stay one day or three days or seven days, and, at the end, the host Da Derga will say, ' Haste ye back. A great pity that it is not coming ye are instead of going ! ' ''

'' Wait you ! '' said Tulchinne the Pict. '' Food there may be in plenty, but no spoil where there is no toll.''

'' No man pays toll, that is true, but men—and some women—have a way of their own in giving. A poor man will leave behind a good story and a good wish, a poet the words of a song or a hand harp wrought in gold and ivory, a horseman his silver spurs or head chain of gold links, a soldier a shield with golden studs, a princeling a torque of gold or a bracelet or a brooch, a woman a silken web or a tapestry—other things. I cannot tell you all, the house and the walls of the house are so plenished. Hear ye the presents Conaire the King sent Da Derga after an entertainment of eight days and eight nights : one hundred kine, one hundred swine, one hundred mantles close woven, one hundred swords blue-bladed, ten red-gold brooches, ten vats of brown ale, ten thralls, ten querns, three brace of white hounds in silver leashes, and three white stallions to outrun the deer. It was I that took the presents to Da Derga's door, and I know."

"A story grows in the telling," said Tulchinne meaningly, "and it is not the first time Fer Rogain told it—so glib he was."

"Cut it in three," murmured Flann, "but it is still the present of a King."

"I have told ye," said Fer Rogain, and turned to Ingcel. "That is the house I offer for your destruction."

Lomna Druth lifted up his voice and his mad eyes.

"Wo! Wo! a terrible thing you do, brother."

"A terrible thing we did to Ingcel. That house is his."

"And all—all in it?"

"To the mouse at the fire-nook."

"Oh wo! oh wo! What do I see?"

"Wait you—wait you!" Tulchinne protested. "We did not come the long salt road to buy a pig in a bag's bottom. Could it be that this man of the hostel is himself a giver of presents?"

"With both hands."

"Easy come, easy go! There might not be

many shields with gold bosses, or gauds for a woman's neck."

"Let Ingcel decide."

"How am I to decide, Fer Rogain?"

"The only way. Send a light-footed man you can trust to look inside the house in every room."

"That is a fair way," agreed Ingcel after a pause.

"I will land your man across there in the sand-hills before the dawn, and send the three red men of Cualla to guide him. They know the road and they know me, and they know the high hills of Alba will not hide them if the sons of Donn Desa are looking for them with the sword's point."

The three red brothers laughed, and Clotach crossed his fingers.

"I do not mind your sword's point, Fer Rogain, but, by my father's fingerbones, I will keep faith. I speak for my brothers, too."

"Listen now, Ingcel!" went on Fer Rogain. "When your looker is on the road we will cross the bay to a cove I know, hidden below the rocks, and from there I will lead you among empty woods and hills to a secret place at the end of the glen above the hostel. You know the Hollow-of-the-Thrushes, Clotach?"

"I know it well, Fer Rogain."

"Heed you then! The night that is coming, or the night after—but not later—you will lead

Ingcel's man to us at that place, and if Ingcel is not pleased with the word brought we have Naas-na-Righ below us, and all fat Leinster.''

And after another considering pause Ingcel said :

'' That is a good plan.''

'' Choose your man then.''

And after another while Ingcel spoke in a low voice without turning his head :

'' It is said that a woman in her beauty, a jewel in her open hand, may walk unafraid the roads of Erin.''

'' It is near enough the truth,'' said Fer Rogain smiling.

'' A man with one hand and a staff of ash is safe most roads ? ''

'' But not safe for a treacherous act at the road's end,'' said Flann behind Ingcel's shoulder.

'' Someone I must send,'' said Ingcel patiently, '' and one from the rich land south of the Four Seas is a good judge of wealth.''

No one but Ingcel heard Flann's voice.

'' I warn you not to trust me, Ingcel.''

'' I have done that already in this game we play together.''

'' But not in this. Trust these red men, but I will not tie my one hand in any bond. I tell you now that, if it pleases me, I will warn the keeper of the Hostel of the thing in store.''

"You were sent to me," said Ingcel still patiently, "and if that is the end for which you were sent I will abide it." He lifted his voice. "You will go."

"I will go to Da Derga's house," said Flann. "What does it matter?"

Lomna Druth's mad eyes glared at him.

"You will go, one-hand, and you will betray princes, and you will be my fifth between wide doorposts."

"Where your body walks three steps without a head, madman."

## CHAPTER XV.

### *Flann of the Left Hand Buys a Bargain.*

FLANN and his three red men of Cualla marched leisurely southward on the level chariot road that flanked Mid Luchair.

The talk went frankly and amicably amongst them, and there was laughter, though it was not Flann's laughter. These three red hounds, Clotach and Cetach and Conal, were not men used to the sea, and were so glad to be on firm land again that they could not help boasting of the noble bloody reiving they had done in these parts.

Flann was as frank and as mordant as they were. He looked about him at the groves of oak and ash and whitethorn that came down to the margin of the road, and, said he :

"If the King's guards met ye now they would not have to look far for a tree."

Clotach laughed, and Cetach and Conal laughed with him. They were three of one birth, but Clotach, by some force in him, was the leader. What he did the other two did, and what he thought the other two thought, and what he said the other two had their mouths open to say. So like were they that no man might put his finger on one and name his name.

" One of Conaire's geasas," said Clotach, " is that three red men shall not fare the road before him. If Conaire saw us he would turn back."

" But his guards might have no geasa."

" They would not trouble three poor honest men going the road," said Clotach, and the three brothers laughed.

Flann looked them over. They were surely three red men. Red hair below red helmets, and red necks below red hair ; red stubble on chin, red tunics red-belted, red cloaks to their heels, red shields with bosses of red bronze ; even the white of their eyes was streaked with red, and, when they laughed, their tongues showed red as cherries.

" For men of your trade," said Flann, " you have marked yourselves to make sure of a hanging."

And again they laughed at him.

" And we the clever ones !" boasted Clotach.

" Clever ones ! " echoed the two.

" When we are at our own trade we do not wear red at all, and a handful of soot on the face has its own hiding."

" All the same, not many wolves die of old age on a rock in the sun. Fer Rogain knows ye."

"So he does. That time he took Conaire's presents to Da Derga we made an onfall on him for toll, but a stallion threw Conal, and Fer Rogain caught him and washed his foolish face. But Fer Rogain does his own share of reiving."

"Some day, with sober years on him, he might remember whose foster-brother he is, and go looking for you with a piece of rope—or three pieces of rope."

"We keep minding that, and minding it—years might not come on him."

"I know ye, too."

"And that is a strange thing. But you are only a foreign man with one hand going the road with a stick. Moreover, we would have a cure for you, too, and you looking sideways at us, your mouth open."

"We know where we stand now," said Flann.

Some time about noon the road turned out of the woods to the crown of a pleasant green valley where a trickle of water hasted and sang down the slope to add its mite to a broad river that wound in wide curves between alders and clumps of sallagh. Directly below, the water ran brokenly over the gravel of a ford, and beyond the ford the white road lifted straight over the brae into the woods that crowned the valley's lip.

"That is the water of Liffe," said Clotach,

" and there runs our own road of Cualla. We will eat here."

They sat by the rivulet and ate cold mutton, and cupped the water in their hands for a drink. And as they chewed and talked there came to their ears the thin squeal of a swine. They turned to see a man and a woman come out of the wood round a copse of hazel.

The man was in the lead, and he was a thin, wiry small man, with wicked black eyes, and a mane of ragged, black-grizzled hair, and a black-grizzled ragged beard, and rags for clothing. In his left hand he held the end of a straw rope, and the other end of it was tied to the hind leg of a small black swine that persistently squealed its protest as it was dragged along. And in his right hand he held the end of another straw rope, and the other end of that one was tied on the waist of a woman, and a young woman, that made no protest but walked sullenly, head down, and with black tossed hair hiding her eyes.

The three red brothers laughed mockingly together.

" Ho-ho-ho ! Fercal the Black and his black daughter ! "

And Clotach shouted : " He-oro, Fercal ! Is your Cicuile still on your hands ? "

The black man came closer, his black eyes snapping wickedly.

"Cheap she is going, the bitch!" said he, and the squeak of his voice was as angry as the swine's, and worse-tempered. "Will you make me a bid for her, Conal—or is it Cetach?"

"The third time and you will get it. A bid for her, Fercal boy? This leg-bone of a sheep with most of the meat on it."

"That is no offer," squeaked Fercal. "Give me something I can turn into meat to-morrow and the day after, for a year and a day."

"Sit down and try your teeth anyway."

Fercal caught the bone that was thrown at him, sat on his spare calves and bared his teeth, but, before his teeth could clamp in the meat, the small black swine jerked on the straw rope, and the bone fell on the grass. The man yelled with fury, clawed at the bone, wiped it hastily on his ragged thigh, and kicked the swine with his bare toes; and the swine's protest was no more furious than the man's. Thereafter he tied the straw rope to an ash sapling, and crouched and gnawed and gulped like a man sharp-edged with hunger. The other straw rope he held in the crotch of a knee and the girl leant against the sapling, her eyes on the ground and her hair over her eyes; and the small black swine nuzzled her shin bone.

The three red brothers drew in their breaths after great laughter and wiped their red eyes with red knuckles.

Flann, who had not laughed at all, rose to his feet, took his last mutton bone out of his satchel, and paced four slow paces to the girl.

" Eat ! " he said briefly.   And she took the bone without lifting her eyes and without thanks.

She turned her head aside to eat, and, though hunger was ravening in her, she bit daintily and chewed slowly, holding the bone up and looking at it through her hair.   Flann leant on his ashen staff and looked at her.

She was young and tall—nearly as tall as he was—and she was built for strength and speed.   A dark girl with a mop of black hair that the sun of twenty summers had not rusted, and through the tendrils of it on her brow he caught a side glimpse of sullen brown eyes.   She was wearing a knee-length, shapeless smock of hodden grey, rent and soiled, but the shapelessness of it could not hide the firm set of her shoulders, the fullness of her young breast, the long, lithe lines of hip and thigh. Her legs were bare and brown, and her strong feet were bare, too, and had been washed that morning.   But her face had not been washed for a week or ten weeks.   It was a woefully dirty face.   The grime had set in the hollows at each side of the nostril, below her chin, below her ears, in the shell of her ears, in the pits of her eyes, and there was one new black smudge across the bridge of her nose and her cheeks.   A young, strong, slattern wench, with a wide mouth that might be generous if it were not so desperately sullen! But she ate daintily, and her hands were not dirty.

That is what Flann saw. But, indeed, no! Flann of the bitter wisdom saw more than that. Behind the dirt, behind the terrible, hopeless sullenness of mouth and eyes and side-turned head, he sensed fear, and behind the fear some enduring, watchful spirit that held her shoulders straight and hid something to be guarded desperately. A strange feeling near to pity stirred with a numb pain in his heart, and his sombre, lean face darkened as he turned away to look down on black Fercal crunching away at the gristle of his bare bone.

" Is she your daughter, black snake? "

" The daughter of the woman that was my wife, horse-face."

The red men laughed. " Watch his tongue, Flann! "

Flann remained ominously calm.

" You would sell her? " he asked curiously.

" I would—even to a man with one hand."

" Why? "

" Because I must eat, and no longer will she work for me." He grew angrier. " For four weeks and five weeks now she will not do a hand's turn though I beat her dawn and dusk—and in the night when I wake out of a bad dream."

" You beat her? "

"I do so, and to show you—and a price for this bone—I will beat her before your eyes as soon as the strength of it gets into me."

"There will be a beating," said Flann softly, and went deep into a thought of his own. Then he asked :

"What is your price ? "

Black Fercal looked up and over him with knowing, beady black eyes. He noted the plain brown cloak, the plain leather belt on the saffron tunic, the brown arms without bracelets, the swordless hip ; but, instead of sword, the hip carried a satchel that did not look to be empty, and a small hope lifted in Fercal's greedy heart.

"My price ! You heard it. What will keep me in meat for a year and a day."

"Why not salt and eat your swine ? "

"You stranger fool ! That cannot be done. That is her dowry. She must have a dowry. It is the custom. And mind you ! that pigeen is of the best breed in Meath, out of Conaire's woods. The mother of that one had twelve to every litter twice a year. A fine dowry ! "

"If you washed her face you might have a better chance of your price."

"I know it ! " he squealed. "Do I not know it ? It is the one thing I cannot get her to do, and my strength going with the years. But, still, I can beat her."

He looked as tough and wiry as a gad of wood-bine, and he had kicked the black swine with the liveliness of youth.

Flann kept looking at the venomous dark man, and the man's nose twitched and his beady eyes fluttered before that calm scrutiny.

"It is his due," said Flann to something in his own mind, and turned to one of the reds.

"You are Clotach?" He was beginning to know Clotach.

"To be sure."

Flann touched the tip of his staff on a red-gold twisted band boss-hooked on Clotach's red-haired wrist. There was a similar band on his other wrist. He had taken the two, and more besides, off a woman at Ormlyth.

"Ingcel will give me my share of the spoil of Ormlyth if I ask him," said Flann. "Give me these two ropes of gold, Clotach, and you can have that share."

"They are yours and welcome," said the generous, careless, red reiver, his hand at a boss. "Say no more about this share and that share." He grinned. "Man, O man! are you for making the bad bargain?"

"Some of it might please you, since you laugh easily."

He thrust one bracelet into his satchel, and he threw the other at Fercal's feet.

" There is your price ! "

Fercal snatched it from the grass, looked at it closely, felt the gold solid weight of it, and then his eyes, all greed, sought Flann's satchel.

" The other one as well ? "

" Give me back that armlet ! " Flann took a stride at him.

" No-no-no ! " squealed Fercal, fumbling the armlet into his breast and scrambling to his feet. " The bitch is yours and the swine with her," and he put a quick twist of the straw rope over Flann's hook.

He took two short steps and poised to leap the runlet, but the iron hook of Flann's staff caught smartly in his rags and held him.

" Be in no hurry, black snake ! " said Flann grimly. " You are not yet paid in full."

So holding Fercal he turned to the girl.

" What is your name ? "

She did not seem to hear him. She was done eating, and grease was about her mouth, but she had wiped her fingers on her stained smock. She leaned against the sapling that was no suppler than she was, her black hair over eyes that were turned sullenly on the ground. Flann gave a quick jerk to the straw rope and set his mind on her like the point of a sword, and his words pierced with the point.

" Answer ! Your name is Cicuile ? "

" It is the name he calls me." Her voice was low, remote, vibrant, out of a young throat.

" It is your name ? "

" My name ! My mother that is dead called me Dairne, but many names I call myself in my own mind."

" Lady—princess—queen—loved one ! The thing we all do in our own minds ! I will call you what your mother called you : Dairne."

" That is my name—Dairne ! "

" Listen to me, O Dairne ! " A small jerk on the rope. " You are strong and young. Why did you let him beat you ? "

" He is my father."

" Your half-father. Why did you let him beat you ? "

" It is his right. It is the custom. He beat me always." She was sullen again.

" It is his right no longer."

She had nothing to say to that. It hardly reached her mind.

" Listen, Dairne ! " Again the rope jerked. " I bought you from him with gold."

" Then you will beat me ? "

" I will not beat you."

" I would rather that you beat me only," she murmured desolately.

" Look at me, Dairne ! "

She looked at him quickly through her hair and looked down again.

"Look into my eyes, woman!" And he jerked the straw rope so sharply that she straightened from the sapling. That stern snap in his voice made her toss her head up and her hair off her brow that was broad and white. Her eyes met his, and meeting they held. Brown eyes they were and hazed with dream, possessed with the secret, wistful dreaming that was the only thing of comfort in all her life.

"Listen now!" said Flann, that very patient man. "I paid for you with gold and I will not beat you. You hear me?"

"I hear you, master."

"I will not beat you, but there is one thing you must do for me here and now. One thing!"

"What is that thing, master?"

"Give this man one of his own beatings."

"That man, Fercal?" One gleam came to the surface of the brown eyes.

"This man Fercal. He is nothing to you any more. Give him one of his own beatings."

"It is an order?"

"It is an order."

"I will do that," said Dairne that had been Cicuile, and snapped the rope at her waist with the ease of her young strength.

Black Fercal at the first word of that beating tore his rags free from the iron horn of the staff, jumped the streamlet handy as a boy, and scurried towards the shelter of the hazel copse.

Quick as a rabbit he was, but Dairne was faster than a hound. In ten paces she was up with him, took the dodging turn with him, buffeted him twice on the same ear. He whirled round at her, a rat's squeak in his yell, and slashed and clawed at her with hooked hands. But she was lively and lissome and young, and his hands slashed through empty air. He took two more buffets, staggered, recovered, and kicked at her with evil intent. But she drew in her middle with the whip of a bow, neatly caught his foot in the air and brought him down with a clump on his spine-end. His screech rent the air, and, before he could screech again, she flapped him over on his face like a fish in a pan.

She pounced on him.

That was a beating. It was a madness of beating. It was an ecstasy of beating. There was never a beating like it before nor since. Her hands, her knees, her feet pranced and pummelled wherever they could reach, and sometimes all together. They were in a haze of dust and shoutings, but she made no sound at all other than the thumpings. He made enough for the two, and the small black swine added its squealings, and the three reds of Cualla joined in with strangled, joyous yells. The laughter of the three red men hurt them; they kicked their heels, lay on their backs, sat up again, grasped their ribs, exploded, hooted, wheezed, grew entirely helpless with laughter.

But Flann looked on, still as a stone, and he did not laugh at all. He did not even smile. His long face was serious and sad, and his eyes watchful.

The yells of the beaten one turned to groans, and Dairne's hands were weary of pummelling. But the long-mounting madness of revolt in her was not half glutted. She sank her fingers in his mat of grizzled black hair, and began steadily thumping his face into the grass, and, lucky for him, the grass was a thick felt. And there Flann dropped his staff, leaped the stream, and set his bronze hook in the neck of her grey smock. It took all his strength to pull her away from her victim, for she strained with all of hers to stay by the good work and finish it.

"One beating! One, I said!" he cried at her. "Another will end him. Easy now!"

Still she strained against the hook, but he swung her round, steadied himself, and touched Fercal with an urgent toe. Fercal was no more than whimpering now, his face snuggled into his shoulder, and his hands clasped above his head.

"Up and run! I cannot hold her for ever."

Fercal looked sideways under a hand, and saw the limber force of her aleap on the hook.

"Grip her!" He found his voice to yell. "Grip her! Give me a start." He scrambled half-upright, felt in his breast for his gold band, and made a stooping bolt for the copse of hazel. On the edge of it he turned, lifted up his hands, and started to curse. But Dairne, at that, so nearly tore free from Flann's hook, that Fercal's first curse changed to a yelp, and he turned and dived like a coney into the copse. And there was the end of him.

The new flame of madness in Dairne was not nearly quenched. Having beaten one man, who, all her days, had beaten her of right, she did not now fear any man and hated them all. And here was a man holding her, with a bronze hook pressing at her breast. She swung round at him, a murky flame in her eyes instead of sullenness, her white teeth bare.

"Let me go!" she cried, and struck at him with clawing fingers. A bead of blood came out on his cheek and trickled to his long jaw.

"You would beat me, too?" he said, and his left hand caught her right wrist.

"You and all men for ever." Exultant her voice to match the flame in her eyes.

"Beat me then." A challenge, no longer an order.

"I will tear your heart with my teeth."

And that thing she set herself to do. And the three red brothers, not yet sated, cheered her on.

But Flann, for all that he had only one hand, was no weakling. Not a great swordsman, and so unlike his brother Delgaun, and lacking Delgaun's explosive force, yet, as in Delgaun, there was knotted in his lean body some tough iron quality that was indestructible. Dairne's young and abounding energy found itself opposed to that iron force, and the force kept drawing itself and mounting up and closing in about her. She hurled herself against him, her lithe legs twined in his, but he propped his legs firmly, and in one steady, slow stiffening broke her grip like breaking a vine. She slashed at him with her left hand, but he dropped head below shoulder and her blows brushed his hair. She tried to bite his wrist above the bronze hook, but the hook propped her chin.

Already half winded, in five minutes the girl was spent with her own fury. Flann loosed her wrist, held her at the stretch of his right arm, his bronze hook below her chin where the tough grey cloth had torn. Her arms hung at her side, and her thighs sagged. Flann drew three long breaths, and he needed them.

"You cannot beat me, Dairne," he told her. "You cannot beat a man with one hand." He nodded at her, holding her eyes with his. "That is not the way to win the game you play, and to drive the lesson home I am going to break my word and give you my first beating."

"Beat me then!" Her head drooped on her breast, and before it drooped Flann saw the old sullen, patient look quench the last of the fire in her eyes.

"Here is the beating for you," said Flann, and three times he slapped her on the cheek. Not hard slaps nor yet gentle. Steady, even smacks, with a slow, soothing draw of palm following each.

"You are beaten," said Flann.

She waited, and then looked up at him, her eyes strangely vacant.

"You will not be beaten any more." He nodded at her and looked at his palm. "Pah! Dirty one! Why did you soil your young face?"

And he heard her remote whisper :

"That my body stay clean."

"That is a way, too, but it is not a good way." He held her there, his half-shut eyes considering her. "There is another way that is more in woman's mode, and if I had time I would tell you of it. Come with me now!"

She followed the draw of his bronze hook, dumb and quiet as a beaten hound. And one of the red brothers called a merry question after them.

A little way down the slope the runlet toppled

164

over a boulder and made a pleasant tinkle into a limpid small basin. There Flann halted her.

"Down." And she went to her knees under the press of his hand, and then down on her hands with her face above the water, and her eyes looking up brokenly at her three inches below her nose.

Flann bestrode her, so that his knees gripped behind her arms, and slowly, firmly drove her head under until the water flowed against his wrist and her hair swayed sideways with the flow of the stream. Her head remained passive under his hand. He counted five slowly and brought her up to gasp, and as she gasped her head jerked against his palm. She looked up at him, the water making lines in the soot on her cheeks.

"Do not torture me, man-of-no-ruth," she besought him pitifully. "Hold my head under till I die. I was always afraid to face death."

"Poor foolish one!" said Flann sadly, and sadness in him. "I only wash your face."

She looked down into the water and moved her head under his hand.

"That will be bad as death for me."

"It might be worse for someone else before all is done," Flann told her, and set to work.

He made a complete job of that face-washing. He took off cloak and tunic to it, remembering days long gone when his own face had needed washing and his mother had done it with a knowledge of all

165

the tender spots. In a side-whirl of the little pool was a pocket of clean sand, and with that he scrubbed her, and his hand was not light. Head and face he scrubbed and re-scrubbed her, and, dumbly patient, she bore the rough cleansing, keeping her eyes and her mouth shut and turning her head this way and that for him. When he moved the hair aside from her neck he saw that it was clean, and the soft swelling of her breast below the tear in her smock was whiter than curd.

At last, critically examining the shells of her ears and the pits of her nostrils, he was satisfied. With the clean inside of his tunic he patted the water off face and throat, and rubbed furiously into her hair, and her hair, as the water left it, bunched up into curls under his hands. And a surprising thing, when he was drying out the whorl of her ear she gave a little soft gurgle.

" You tickle me."

And Flann straightened up, his knees gripping behind her arms, and looked straight before him, a wonder in his face. And after a time he said :

" It might be the duty of a man to make her laugh often."

He loosed the grip of his knees and stepped over her ; and she sat back on her heels and, with the tips of her fingers curiously felt the clean smoothness of her cheeks. He slipped on tunic and cloak, belted his satchel, and took from it Clotach's gold band.

" Here, Dairne ! "

She came to him at once, and humbly, her head down and black curls on her white, broad brow. He set his hook over her right wrist and pushed her loose sleeve above her elbow. Her arm was clean and white and smooth and round and strong, but above the elbow were two darkening marks where fingers had gripped her roughly. Over these two marks he clasped the gold band of Ormlyth and pulled the sleeve down over it.

" That is yours, Dairne," he told her, and patted her sleeve.

" You give it to me, master ? " and wonder was in the eyes she lifted.

" Not master ! I give it to you. Some day—I do not know—it may be, that some day it will buy you the clean life you look for—if you keep on looking for it."

He was about to turn away when she stopped him with her hand.

" Wait, master ! It is my turn now." And her mouth lost its sullenness in something that was not so much a smile as a small wistful softening.

She leaned to the pool, cupped water in her palm, and gently patted his cheek and jaw where the blood she had drawn from him was dry. He let her do it, and watched the way she turned her head aside—like a child or like a mother—to make sure that her work was well done. But suddenly he flung his head up in a spurn, turned from her, and went long-striding up the slope to where the three red brothers sat on the grass, quiet now, sated with laughter.

Then he glanced back over shoulder. Dairne was standing where he had left her. She had drawn her sleeve up, and was turning her arm this way and that to see the brave, graceful thing it was below its band of gold.

"She is a woman after all," remarked Clotach in some surprise.

"I saw that before you did, Clotach," Flann told him. He knew the speaker was Clotach, because on each red-haired wrist was a ring of white where the gold band had clasped. And Clotach looked at him, a new respect in his red-brown eyes.

"A pleasanter time I never spent. You have a lively mind all your own, Flann-one-hand, and the skill to use it in a new way. I was mistaken in you, and I thinking you a sour-faced man with one hand going the roads of the world on a stick. I am thinking I was a fool not to see that the great Ingcel one-eye had a reason of his own, and a good one, to make you his other eye, and that you had strength enough to deny him." He looked behind Flann's shoulder. "And another thing I am

thinking, and it is this : you did not make such a
bad bargain with my two twists of gold."

Dairne had come quiet-footed up the slope, and
now stood behind Flann where the small black swine
was tethered to the sapling. And the small black
swine grunted softly, and softly nuzzled the back
of her knee.

And indeed she might be the good part of
a bargain, as such bargains go. Her face, clean
above the round young neck, fitted her strong and
shapely body. There was the colour of young
blood there, and a soft duskiness kissed by the sun
that had done the only ardent kissing ; and her
mouth, grave now, but not sullen, hinted its own
generosity, and the make of it for laughter or for
grief ; and her eyes, brown as the eyes of a noble
hound, were spaced wide and deep below black
brows on a white, broad forehead where black
curls clustered.

"Let me see now," said Clotach, that sound
judge, rubbing his stubble consideringly. " Put a
long green kirtle on her, with open sleeves silver-
tasselled, and red shoon peeping below the green,
and a red belt on her hips, and a red selvedge low
on her neck, and a white silver band on her hair,
and you will sell her to a prince for your two fistfuls
of gold, and gold running over—if selling her you
will be."

" I will buy her," said one of the brothers.

"Where are your fistfuls, Conal?" enquired Clotach derisively.

"I will give this for her," said Conal. He was on his feet, his fingers feeling at the broad three-quarter circle of a gold-and-bronze brooch holding his red cloak at the shoulder.

"She is not mine to sell," said Flann, and turned to the girl. "Will you take the brooch, too, Dairne?"

She tossed her head with a woman's new disdain, and found her woman's tongue.

"Him! He is only Conal of Cualla, who with his brothers steals goats and swine in the dark and the dawn, a black cloak on him and soot on his face. I mind the soot and the way it added ugliness to ugliness."

Flann lifted his long chin and laughed, and he was a man that did not laugh often.

"Only Fer Rogain knew the trade ye follow!" he said witheringly. "Here is a young one of the woods can hang ye with a word."

"There is a cure for her, too," said Conal, "and it is not the cure that Clotach spoke about that other time. Tell me, Cicuile—or is it Dairne?—how did you know that I was a robber by night?"

"I saw you at it often and I lying under a bush."

"And you let your tongue say it to Fercal in the

morning—to others maybe? " His voice was velvety.

She moved her head slowly. " I did not speak it to anyone."

" My wise one ! But what were you doing under the bush ? "

" I was listening to what the birds were saying, their head from below their wings."

" And you knowing the birds' tongue ? "

" I know the voices in all the woods. I know what my small swine is saying to me now, nuzzling my knee."

" What is he saying to you ? "

" He is saying, ' Come, O Queen ! Come ! Acorns under trash.' "

" The very thing a porker would say," said Conal agreeably. " I have great hearing myself—I have the greatest hearing in the world—but lack skill in tongues. You will be very useful to me. Here, Flann, is my fine brooch for you, and I would give you more if I had it."

He thrust the brooch at Flann, but Flann struck his hand aside with his bronze hook, and the brooch fell on the grass.

" You heard what she said, red man ? "

Conal picked up the brooch, carefully reset it at his shoulder, and then faced Flann, his eyes level, and his hand on the hilt of his short bronze sword.

" It is the first time I offered to buy what I could

take, and it is the last. I will take her, one-hand."

But Clotach was on his feet now.

"Conal, you hound!" he roared with all his might. "Flann bought her fairly with my gold bands, and by the fingerbones of my father and your father, she is his to keep or sell. Sit down, dog!"

He thrust his clenched fist against Conal's breast, and Conal sat down suddenly at the side of his brother Cetach, who laughed at him.

"You never had any luck, red fool," said Cetach.

Conal looked up at Clotach and grinned without malice.

"Whatever you say, brother, and sure the year is long."

But sitting down, his arms propping him, he stiffened in that posture, his head stiff, and one ear turned listening towards the curve of the road behind.

"H-s-s-t! Listen, O listen! Do ye hear?"

## CHAPTER XVI.

### *The Tabu is Broken.*

THEY all listened, their mouths open to aid their ears. But, except Conal, they heard nothing; and then they found that they heard a good deal: the chuckle of water over stone, the whisper of air in young leaves, the caw of a rook far away, all the small sounds of the wood. But they did not hear at all what Conal was hearing.

"What do you hear, man-of-one-gift?" asked Clotach.

"The gift of hearing, that is what I have," said Conal proudly. "I can hear the grass growing, the rustle of a hedgehog at the foot of a bush, the whistle of a bat in the evening, the song of one midge in the sun——"

"What do you hear, Conal the boaster?" Clotach used a toe firmly.

"Wait now and I will tell." He lay flat and set an ear to the ground, his face vacant of all expression, and his eyes turned inward in a blind squint. Then he began to murmur in slow spaced words :

" Horses—many horses—and men with easy voices—wheels—chariots clanking on bronze axles wagons slurring on wood. A hound barked that time—there is the crack of the hunter's whip—you heard the yelp ? "

" I heard it," said Dairne. The others heard nothing.

" A big company," said Conal, and sat up. " A big company on the road and coming this way ; a long way off—from here to that further brink, and twice as far again."

Conal and Cetach looked at Clotach questioningly, and he answered their look.

" If the company is big there is nothing in it for us, and nothing to fear in it either—three honest red men at the edge of their own road. Not many know that we went the sea way with Fer Rogain."

" Wait ye ! " cried Cetach. " I have my gift, too. I can see the colour of the wind like a swine sees it. It is red. I can see anything that is above the curve of the ground, and the colour of a man's eyes, his head no bigger than a crab. Ye know that." He was boasting, too. " From the head of Uisneach I can look abroad and see Indeoin, Cult, Cuilten, Mafat, Ammat, Iarmafat, Finne, Goiste, Guestine——"

Clotach sent him staggering with a thrust.

" Go and see what you can see now. The road runs a straight mile from that birch at the corner. Run ! "

Cetach ran fleet and silent as a hound on the grassy margin of the road, threw himself flat behind the birch, and craned his neck out and up. He looked steadily for all of a minute, got slowly to his feet, had one last look to make sure, and came running back to them. There was awe in his face, and there was the beginning of a fear at something that his mind touched and started away from.

" A splendid lofty cavalcade making the land shake—a full hundred," he panted. " Bright spears over chariots—ivory hilts to swords—silver shields on elbows, garments all the seven colours—horses foray-nimble——"

" Who is it ? " Clotach's voice rasped.

" It is himself. It is Conaire the High King on his white stallion, with his young son at his side, and MacEcht and Conall Cernach riding at each shoulder."

" Fingerbones of my father ! " swore Clotach, and looked up into the sky. " Where does Conaire my king fare ? "

" To the Hostel of Da Derga," Flann answered him calmly and promptly.

" No-no-no ! " cried Clotach vehemently. Yet he put Cetach a quick question : " Are they all fighting men ? "

" Half—not a half.   Charioteers, huntsmen,
playboys—the retinue he travels with."

" Fifty fighting men—not many."

" Not many against eight hundreds," said
Flann.   " But where then does this King ride if
not to the Hostel? "

" To the King of Leinster at Naas-na-Righ,"
said Clotach, holding his mind away from his fear.

" Where else might he ride? "

Clotach, the resolute one, answered that.

" You said it.   To the Hostel of Da Derga—
there is no other place."

" That is where he rides."

" You do not know, one-hand? "

" I do not, but it fits.   Everything that has
happened fits in its own place, and mad Lomna
Druth was right.   Your King of Tara is riding to
his doom, and Fate is about him."

" If Fate is in this," said Clotach resolutely,
" we are in it, too, and Fate has a finger on us."
He turned to his brothers.   " Conal, you have the
gift of hearing ; and you, Cetach, the gift of sight ;
but there is my gift, too.   I have the gift of understanding.   I know what to do."

" We do what you do," said the brothers
together.

" Listen then !  We will be Conaire's geasa once
again : three red men faring before him to the

house of Da Derga, who is a red man, too, and when Conaire sees us he will turn back."

" If he does not turn back ? " That was Flann.

" He will take the fork to Naas-na-Righ when he sees us take the one to the Bruden."

" And if he follows ye, breaking his geasa ? "

" We can do no more," said Clotach, changing his feet.

" You, Clotach, can, and you can do it here. Your feet are restless, and you know what you can do. Wait here for Conaire and warn him. It will not be hard for him to raise a force to scatter the reivers."

" It will not be hard at all," agreed Cetach and Conal together.

Clotach walked three paces away and three back, and said he :

" You are forgetting, one-hand, that I crossed fingers for Fer Rogain. I cannot open my mouth. I am bound. And I bind ye, too, red whelps."

" I am not bound," said Flann quietly.

" That is true," said Conal hopefully. " I heard you, and you whispering that very thing to Ingcel. You could do the warning ? "

" I could, and I might," agreed Flann derisively. " But instead I might tell Fer Rogain to-night— or to-morrow night—when I come to him in the glen. Fer Rogain would never let Ingcel destroy the Hostel if Conaire is there."

But Clotach only shook his head.

" You can try. But Fer Rogain is bound, too, and I know the iron in him. Are you forgetting that Ingcel's father was slain, and his seven brothers? But you can try."

" I know the iron of Ingcel," said Flann. " I will follow my road as I see it."

" We know ours. Come, brothers! " He gathered them to him with his strong arms. " We will cross the Liffe River and go up the road of Cualla. Slow and slower we will go until Conaire sees us, and then make for the fork to the Bruden before him." He looked over his shoulder at Flann. " You will do and say what you like, Flann one-hand. There is a liking for you growing in me, and I warn you that there is a geasa for the king in yourself and the woman you own. Hide ye under a bush till Conaire turns back."

" Or till he rides by, following you? "

" Follow after, keeping out of sight, and you will know the road he takes. Come, brothers! "

The three, arm in arm, went long striding down the brae, and splashed across the ford ; and arm in arm they set foot on the white road of Cualla, and marched slowly and more slowly upwards. Their bright red cloaks fell to their heels, and their red helmets took the sun redly. They were three red men, surely.

" It is time we hid, master," came Dairne's low

voice behind Flann's shoulder. "They are very near."

Flann came up out of his thoughts and turned towards the road corner.

He could hear the soft thud of horses' hooves in the dust, the clink of harness chains, the clack of axles, a murmuring voice or a voice raised.

"There is that hazel bush, master," urged Dairne. "We must hurry."

"Hide then. And if Fercal lurks give him your own beating."

"You will not hide, master?"

"I would, but my feet are tied. I will look at this Conaire that is called great, and, if a part is set for me to play, I will try to play it."

Her own fear shook Dairne's shoulders. She placed a hand on the straw rope that tethered the swine, looked from Flann to the hazel bush and back again, and then she said with a tremor:

"I will try not to hide this time."

"That is a great bravery," said Flann a little bitingly, and the bite she gave him back had teeth in it.

"There is a traitor's thought in your mind, master."

"There is," he agreed, "but there is another thought, too." And he went on half musing. "There is the thought of Ingcel, that strong man, set on fathering a son of his own in the land of the

Picts. There is a liking in me for Ingcel one-eye.
I am a great fool, Dairne."

" I think that is what you are, master."

" Be not one yourself," he said shortly. " Will
you warn the King for me ? "

" If you bid me, master."

" You obey me in all things," he said sourly,
and turned from her.

Dairne went and crouched against the ash
sapling, drew the black swine close under one arm,
curled her legs under her smock, and shook the
shapelessness of it on her breast. Then she plucked
out a tuft of grass with black clay at its roots, and
lifted it for the besmirching of her washed face ;
but before it touched her face, she looked at Flann's
back, sighed, shook her head and threw the tuft
away. She tossed her hair down over her eyes.
Whatever she saw after that she saw through the
tendrils of curling black hair.

Flann stood easily, one footed, on the grass
margin of the road, his chin alean on the iron horn
of his staff, and watched the cavalcade come round
the curve of the road.

One man rode at the head of it on a white stallion.
A young man still, with golden hair flowing free
below a gold band, and a gold-red short beard
curling on his chin. He wore no armour below a
cloak that was dappled with the iridescence of a
peacock's tail and embroidered on one shoulder

with a wide-pinioned white bird brown-spotted, and embroidered on the other with a golden wheel. His face was high and noble and generous and thoughtful, and it was a sad face, too.

" That is Conaire the High King of Erin," said Flann to himself, " and he might be great."

At the King's right thigh a boy of not more than ten springs rode and reined a roan pony ; and, in his boy's mind, he was the gallant great leader of a great army. An open-air young hawk in white and red, with a face all brown freckles, and brown hair with a sheen of red in the sun, but sun-faded to flax at the points.

" The son of a King," said Flann.

Behind the King two men rode together. One was tall and supple, on a tall, slender roan-red horse ; the oblong shield slung at his thigh had a ground the colour of blood and was riveted with bronze studs over plaques of gold ; at the full stretch of his right hand a tall spear with a fluted shaft stood high above his head of red curls. As he rode nearer, Flann saw that one cheek was white as milk unkissed by sun, and the eye over it as coldly blue as a cold sea ; and the other cheek carried the purple-red splash of a birthmark below an eye as dark-blue as a mountain at fall of day.

" Lithe like a panther, that man is known," said Flann.

The other rider, on a heavy black horse, was a

huge, unwieldy man, black from crown to heel—black hair on his bare thighs, black tunic, black cloak, black mat of hair and beard, and his look black and sullen. The leaf-blade of his massive spear was three spans long and one wide, and a wide-mouthed axe hung at his hip.

" Smash or split—it is all the one," said Flann.

Behind the leaders a full score of horsemen rode in a body, but not in order. Amongst them Flann noted three riding together who wore long, lint-white hair on the shoulders of woad-blue linen, and he remembered seeing hair and colour like these in his journey through East Britain.

Ten chariots unscythed, in single file, came next, drawn by white horses. They were bowed with bronze, and the wheels bronze-banded. A charioteer, in white and red livery, sat at ease over one wheel, and a spearman in bronze breastplate over the other.

Behind the chariots, in a soft pother of knee-high dust, three men walked abreast : squat, strong, sallow, blue-bearded men wearing kilts of skin and carrying leather targes.

" Tulchinne the Pict would say, ' Hail, brothers ! ' " was Flann's thought.

Behind the Picts shambled three giants of men with necks and shoulders that had the massive, forward curve of the fighting bull's. They wore short brown kilts and nothing else, and swung great wooden maces studded with iron nails.

"The panther with the red cheek would rend the three for an appetite," said Flann.

Three long wains, behind three pairs of brown horses, came lumbering and creaking on single-piece wooden wheels. They were loaded high with gear under cover, and on the covers men squatted lazily, among them three white-bearded men carrying gilded harps carefully on their laps About and behind the wains many walked in the film of white dust, some in the king's colours of white and red, and some in gay colours of their own. And a gay company they were, with talk and laughter and sly horseplay. At the corner of the road one of them, in tight lissome green, jumped on to the grass, made two lively hops, turned two somersaults and finished with an easy heel-clicking bound.

"The King carries his own entertainment with him," said Flann.

Behind the wains came four huntsmen leading hounds in leash : three pairs of noble brindled wolf-hounds and one pair of slender milk-white greyhounds.

Last of all marched the rearguard : twelve soldiers on foot, bronze helmeted, bronze shielded, armed with bronze-headed spears and bronze swords.

There was no woman in all the company.

What struck Flann most was the wonderful splashing of colour up and down the long line : all the colours of the rainbow and all the blends, with winks and flashings of yellow gold, white silver, red bronze, cream ivory. In all his travels he had not seen anything to equal it, not even among the Romans that came to Rem Hove in their triremes.

The rearguard was at the corner when the King came level with Flann, and Flann caught the flash of the blue eyes as they swept over and past him and looked straight ahead. And what those blue eyes saw ahead made the King check his white stallion and point with a long arm.

" Another of my geasas ! Three red men fore-faring ! I am weary of geasas."

" Time for you, O lord, and the trouble they are to you," said the tall blonde man riding behind the King.

Indeed that was the truth. Fer Rogain had broken one geasa, and then all the other foolish ones had come pelting down on Conaire like hailstones.

South in Thomond two of his Cairbre septs had at last come to the height of a long dispute about boundaries, and when that height is reached, hot blood-flowing follows the next hot word.

" Geasa or no geasa," said Conaire, "I will stop this, and if blood is spilled it is I will spill it."

He rode south with a full retinue of guards and

hostages and entertainers, spent five nights with one sept and five nights with the other, walked the boundaries with them on either hand, and saw them embrace warmly and warily at the end. He had settled their quarrel, and spent more than nine nights out of Tara; and two more geasas were broken.

He rode north then at his ease, round by Uisneach of Meath to come lefthandwise by Tara; but one morning he saw a cloud of smoke out of the woods of Cerna and many half-naked men skirmishing in the smoke. He galloped forward, his sword drawn and his guards deployed, for he feared a raid by sullen old Maeve of Connacht; but it was only a heath fire threatening his woods, and the half-naked men were his foresters fighting the flames. He and his retinue helped till high noon, and had the fire under control when two immense wolves, white-throated, broke from the covert.

Conaire's two pair of brindled wolfhounds were out of leash at the time, and, before anyone might move to stay them, they were on the traces. The chase was on, and the whole retinue, with Conaire leading on his white stallion, galloped yelling. It was a long chase. It lasted all day. It took them righthandwise round Tara, curved away east and south, and brought them lefthandwise round Bregia, and finished at sunset with the bay and the killing on the edge of the chariot road of Mid

Luchair. And when the wolves were dead everyone knew them for the evil beasts of Cerna.

"No loss," said Conaire, laughing. "At this rate there will be no geasas to tie the hands of my little son, Le Fri Flait."

They camped in the woods back from the road that night, and next morning Conaire looked about him.

"I know this road," said he. "At the end of it there is a good friend of mine."

"If you mean Da Derga the Red and his Hostel," said MacEcht, "we could do worse than visit him. He owes us a good hosting."

"And a good one he will give us," said Conaire. "Let us ride."

They rode away south till they came to the open valley of the Liffe River, and there the King drew rein. A lean man in a brown cloak stood on one leg by the margin of the road, his chin resting on the iron horn of a staff of ash. For a right hand he had a polished bronze hook. Behind him a woman in a shapeless grey smock sat acrouch against a sapling, her head down and her black hair hiding her face; and a small black swine was held tight against her side, and bared his young tusks at the snarling hounds.

"The breaking of another geasa here," was Conaire's thought, and he looked across the valley to where the white road of Cualla mounted the slope.

Beyond the river, three men walked abreast up the white road. They were three red men. Red cloaks to their heels, red shields of bronze on left arms, red hair flowing below red helmets, they were, indeed, three red men.

" There goes another of my geasas," said Conaire. " Three red men forefaring to the house of red. I am weary of geasas."

" Time for you, O lord, and the trouble they are to you," said the tall blonde man riding behind the King. " What cure have you for this one? "

" I know the cure I would like, Conall Cernach," said the King bleakly.

The King at halt, the company came closing up. Men moved forward on either side to see what he looked at so sternly across Liffe Water, and when they saw, they looked at each other with frowning eyes and whispered here and there. Tabus had troubled them these many days.

The massive black-bearded man drove his horse to the King's side and thrust his broad-bladed spear at the point.

" I know these three red rogues. They are the one-birth brothers of Cualla, and I have a cure for them as well."

" Fine. I know the sort of cures you have, MacEcht," said the King ironically.

"All I would do is hail them to heel to swallow our dust."

"I could do as much myself, being King, but as a King I cannot put a strong hand on three men going their own road quietly."

"For a long time," persisted the stubborn MacEcht, the King's champion, "there is a suspicion at me that the same three are robbers by night, and deserve a good hanging. Say the word, Conaire, my dear, and I have my own choice of trees."

"My poor fool, MacEcht! I cannot be rid of my geasa by hanging it."

"A better way I never heard of, but you will go your own King's way. Very well so! Let us turn for Tara then, and keep the few geasas that are left."

"It is not luck to turn back either, MacEcht. Moreover, these three red men may not be faring before me to the house of red."

"I will find that out for you in less than no time," said MacEcht, and gathered his reins into his big fist.

"No, army man!" the King stopped him. "You might aid your question with axe poll."

"I will be your messenger, O lord," said the blonde panther whom the King had called Conall Cernach.

"You are of Ulster, Conall, and these three of Leinster might not care for your questioning."

"I would make them care."

"There is one of them named Clotach," growled MacEcht, a sour eye on Conall, "and you would not make him care the longest day in summer."

"Peace, children!" chided the King. "I will send one that will speak and be listened to in courtesy." He leant to the princeling who was looking at him eagerly. "Le Fri Flait, my darling! You will be my messenger."

"I will, my father," piped the lad, and struck his heels into his pony.

But his father grasped the reins at the bridle, bringing the pony to its haunches, and Le Fri Flait swayed from the hips like a horseman.

"Be not hasty, little son! There is your message. Remembering your manners and whose son you are, you will ask these three red men if they fare before us to the Bruden of Da Derga. If that is not the end of their road, bid them their share of luck on whatever road they go, and hasten back——"

The youth tightened his reins, eager to be off.

"Wait now, little one! There is more. If they are for the hostel, say to them: 'My father, your King, requests you to fare in his company and dip finger in the dish with him——'"

"Request, indeed!" growled MacEcht, and the King's impatient hand silenced him.

"Churls, they may spurn you, my son," he went on, "and then you will say to them: 'Go another road, and my father will send you three oxen and three pigs fatted to kill.' If they are robbers, as my champion says, they may want more, and you will say to them: 'Six oxen, six pigs, the leavings of my father's table in the place where he eats, and a seat at the fire corner.' If they refuse that, you will come back and I will not know whether they are churls or robbers or men bound by a geasa. Go now, boy! We will wait here for you."

Like a bolt the eager lad was gone, driving full speed down the slope, splashing water out of the ford, breasting the steep road of Cualla, shoulders forward. The three red men, near the top, saw him come, hastened their slow pace, and disappeared into the trees.

The King sat watching until his son also disappeared over the top, then, shrugging the thought of geasas out of his mind, he threw leg over his horse's withers and slid to the ground. His company, in duty bound, did likewise, and equerries in the king's livery of white and red came forward to hold the horses.

Conaire, with Conall Cernach and MacEcht behind him, stamped about in his soft-tanned yellow riding boots, and in his own time came to the margin of the road where Flann leaned on the horn of his ashen staff ; and Flann gave him the royal salute, open hand palm-down and head forward.

" Man of the roads," spoke the King in his gentle way, " which of the five kingdoms is yours ? "

" I am not of Erin, lord," Flann answered. " I am out of Long Baravais in Rem, south of the Four Seas."

" I have heard of it. You are welcome to Erin." His mouth twitched into a smile. " Are you, too, for the Hostel of Da Derga ? "

And Flann answered evenly :

" I have a duty there, and I do not like it."

" That is an odd thing to say of that hostel." The King looked behind Flann's shoulder to where Dairne sat hidden by her smock and her hair. He frowned before he could help it. " That woman— is she yours—your thrall ? "

" As I stand, O King," said Flann, " I am not sure what she is."

" I know. A riddle that has puzzled many men ! Whatever she is, and whatever the duty you do not like, bring her to the hostel before fall of night. I may not receive a woman after sunset." He smiled. " It is one of the geasas I would like to keep."

Flann's fearless eyes met Conaire's fairly.

"Keep the one that you are now facing, High King of Erin."

"Do you talk to me of geasas, too?" His curled beard lifted under the jut of his stubborn jaw, and his mind refused to be troubled with geasas—on its surface. Instead he contemplated the small black swine against Dairne's side. He was a famous raiser of flocks and droves and knew a good beast when he saw one.

"A shapely young one!" he remarked, nodding towards it.

"Out of your own woods, lord," said Flann. "I will give it to you for your feast."

"My thanks, but I go where high feasting is."

"Nevertheless," said Flann stubbornly, "this young swine cooked and eaten by this running water will be a finer feasting than the feasting before you, and a bed of withered bracken softer than any bed in the Hostel of Da Derga."

The King looked at him long and darkly.

"Are you set there, a man with one hand, standing on one foot, to say that to me?"

Flann remembered how Ingcel had taken him for an omen.

"I am set here, and I say it to you, O King."

The King turned a shoulder to him and looked across the valley to where the road of Cualla topped the brae, and the set of his mouth and jaw was more stubborn than ever.

Conall Cernach, the blonde-red man with the red-splashed cheek, spoke to Flann.

"Baravais in Rem! It is said that great swordsmen live in that place?"

"Great swordsmen are always slain," Flann said.

"Like Naoise—like Cuchulain——"

"Like Conall Cernach some day," rumbled dark MacEcht. "Since the raven perched on Cuchulain's shoulder, where is a greater swordsman than Conall Cernach?"

"I know what is in your mind, MacEcht," said the Ulster hero coldly, "and some day I will put it to the test."

"Any day," said MacEcht readily, "and this day for choice."

"Peace, peace!" said Conaire the King. "Here comes my son, and alone."

Le Fri Flait was riding down to the Liffe River, head down and shoulders hunched, his pony pacing soberly, not galloping now. Flann knew what that meant. So the princeling came to where his father waited, and, before he lifted his head, he shook it, and when he lifted it, the lashes of his eyes were wet.

"Well, small son?" said the King softly.

And Le Fri Flait, holding his voice from trembling, replied :

"They will not come, the three red ones. They—they laughed at me."

" I will mind it for them," said his father. " To laugh at youth is no man's part. Was laughter all, prince ? "

" I gave them your message, father—one, two and three." His words came in a hurry to stem the sobs. " And after each message they laughed at me in one breath, and the man in the middle lifted his head and sang at me. Three times he sang at me, and after the third time he said : ' Remember that singing for your father, our King.' And then they went away from me, running like hounds."

" Is the song in your mind, son of mine ? "

" Some of it, father." And he lifted up the reed of his voice and half-chanted :

> " He-oro, my son,
>  Dark the news !
> In the Hostel of Derga
> Darkness brews.
> Meshed in a net are we three,
> Meshed in that net the King and thee.
> Weary the steed the King doth ride,
> By Liffe Water let him bide.
> We the red ones fare ahead,
> He who follows is soon dead.

Red the signs like our red brows:
  Sating of ravens and hooded crows,
Strife and the wetting of spear edges,
Crash of sword on broken targes,
In the hour of dark when set is sun.
He-oro! Go, my son!"

The young prince looked up into his father's
eyes, and the tears brimmed and ran down his
freckled young cheeks, but he made no sound of
weeping.

"You have done and said your part well, son of
a King," said the father, turning his eyes away
from the tears. He looked across the valley at the
road of Cualla, and his retinue looked at each other
with troubled eyes, and shuffled their feet in the
dust.

"All my geasas are come upon me," Conaire
spoke aloud, but he spoke to himself alone, and
his voice was as stubborn as his jaw. "All my
poor foolish geasas, without meaning and without
purpose! A child tied with cloths between the
legs, not High King of Erin! Bound by rules
made by my dead, I must not make a custom or
break a custom. And yet—and yet! I break my
geasas, and good, not evil, comes of the breaking.
Fer Rogain in exile and rapine under foot, a blood
quarrel settled, my woods saved from fire, the
preying beasts of Cernach slain!—and now?
Must I turn back from visiting a noble friend in

peace because three red men fare before me and threaten me with a song? No king is a man in such trammels. I am a King and will be a man also, and free the feet of my son and sons' sons for all time. I will ride."

He vaulted on his white stallion, threw his arm forward in a curve, and went down the slope at the gallop. The princeling galloped after; MacEcht and Conall Cernach gave heels to their horses; the long train heaved itself slowly into motion and took the pitch of the slope, leather creaking, feet padding, wheels clacking, hounds baying. Here and there men growled and grumbled, but no man raised his voice against the will of Conaire their King and the man they loved.

The deep threat of the wolfhounds was the loudest sound there was, for, when they came abreast of Flann and saw the small black swine at Dairne's side, they strained at their leashes and told the world the things they intended on the carcase of the black one. The whips cracked, the deep clamour lifted to yelping and sank to growling; the six files of the rearguard went stamp, stamp, over the lip of the slope, and the haze of dust cleared away slowly. The bristles of the black pig sank, and he sheated his young tusks. He was a brave small pig, but a prudent one, for he had nestled close to the side of Dairne.

## CHAPTER XVII.

### *Flann Gives Dairne Her Lesson.*

FLANN stayed where he was resting on one foot, his chin on the horn of his staff, and never stirred till the last file had disappeared into the trees on the far rim of the valley ; and Dairne, rising to her feet and tossing her hair out of her eyes, watched them, too. Then Flann spoke.

" In the meshes of one net, surely, and here I take the road to close it—or loose it. I do not know ! I do not know at all ! "

And without a glance behind him, he stepped down into the dust and took two-four strides on the road. Then the shy, servile low voice of Dairne made him pause.

" Your little black pig, master ? "

" Singe him in the pit," he told her shortly over his shoulder.

" But he is your pig, master. That is the custom." She was at his side, and, before he could stop her, had the loop of the straw rope over the bronze hook that did him for a right hand.

Flann looked down at the animal with distaste, and still he found himself smiling ruefully. He had brought this end about with his eyes open, and it was an end that he did not want. As an experiment he put a small strain on the rope, and at once the pig propped its forelegs decisively, and shattered the day with an ear-piercing and persistent squeal. Flann was not silent either. He cursed as hard as he was able and as fast as he could remember. The pig kept on squealing. It was all squeal. Flann lifted a sandalled foot, poised it, chose his spot, hesitated and stamped his foot back in the dust. He thrust the straw rope into Dairne's hands.

" He is your very own pig," he said urgently. " I give him to you. Hold him ! Keep him ! I do not want him. I will not have him. Do not let me see him again. He is your very own darling, damnable small monster. Out of my sight with him ! ''

And he turned and went down the brae in his longest strides. He forged across the ford, not minding the stones that were here and there, and bent to the brae at his best pace ; and he told himself that it was the terror of the pig that drove him. But, half way up, something deep within him made him turn head over shoulder for a last glance. He stopped dead, and his feet turned him round.

There, not six paces behind, Dairne marched

smoothly, easily, lissomely in the silent dust, and the black pig trotted amicably at her side, the straw rope sagging.

"Where are you going, girl?" Flann was stern to hide something akin to fear.

"I am leading your black pig for you, master."

"My black pig? The black demon is yours. Did you not hear me?"

"I heard you, master. But it is against the custom to take back a dowry while life is."

"A great land for custom this," said Flann with restraint. "Where do you think you are going?"

"I will go anywhere you tell me, master, but I cannot take this little black one. That I cannot do, master."

"Master—master! I am not your master. Do not call me master!"

"What must I call you, m——?" Dairne asked mildly, eyes on the ground.

"Call me Flann," he exploded. "Call me one-hand—left-hand—sour mouth—horse-face—fool! Call me anything you like, but not master."

She lifted her eyes, under-brow, at him, and a softening that was not quite a smile touched her mouth and deepened in her eyes.

"Must I choose a name?"

The ironic quirk deepened at the side of one nostril, and he nodded at her.

"I will call you Flann soft-heart," said Dairne gently.

"Flagstones of hell and they hot!" cried Flann soft-heart, his eyes wide but not weary.

"It is the best I could do," whispered Dairne humbly.

"Do not give me the worst, ever." Flann shook his head sadly. "I should have known, but men will never have sense enough not to meddle with a mother's daughter. There are too many mothers behind you, Dairne, for you not to have learned some of your woman's trade. I was a fool. I will be a fool—and not another word need be said."

He swung round and went on his way slowly, his head down, and his eyes on the scuffled dust of the road.

For miles he never looked back, never lifted his head, nor was there any need. The road curved and turned and twisted between great woods, and the tracks of horsemen and footmen, chariots and wagons were easy to follow in the scuffled dust. After a while he let his eyes drift down and behind a shoulder, and saw that Dairne walked silent-footed a pace behind on his right side. Smoothly, easily, firmly her strong bare feet came to the ground, and the grey-white dust gave little soft spurts between the big toe and the toe next it.

"If my brother Maur saw me now with my

woman and my pig," said Flann to himself, "he would make a song that would be sung and laughed at from Rem to the plain of The Ser."

And after a time Flann began to talk aloud, but still as if to himself, and Dairne came close up to his shoulder and listened with all her might. The black pig listened, too, flicking one ear forward in some disdain, but not grunting any dissent.

"This girl, Dairne, I am beginning to know a little. She persists. She is pliant, but she is not to be broken easily. I am afraid of her and for her. The black snake Fercal could not break her, but alas! she will be broken. It could be that she took the only way—the only way she knew—to hold the things she prized. Wild thing of the wood, hearing the wood's tongue, for her no sordid mating. Soot on her nose bridge—and no mighty arch to the same—it has its own hiding. Going humbly, like a mouse shrinking, hair tangle in eyes, fear about her like her shapeless smock, she might escape the seeking eye—for a time. But in time—somewhere—Fercal would make his sordid bargain—and he has made it—he has made it. And is Dairne lucky? Is Dairne lucky?"

"Till she is sold again," Dairne whispered.

"Will she let the grime grow on her face again? Let her try it within reach of my left hand and she will feel the weight of that left hand. That way is closed, for there are three men—or four—who will

remember how Dairne glows beneath the grime.
No! that way cannot avail Dairne any more, for
there are other men who with humility love to play
as a cat plays, and feel their blood stir when fear
grows fearsome before the cat pounces—and the
sun does not always shine. But what other road
may she walk that women have walked, till her day
comes and the night after it? How do I know?
And what do I care?"

His voice had harshened, stopped. He heard
Dairne sigh softly at his elbow. He lifted his
shoulders and dropped them, and remained silent
as long as he could. That was not long.

"A man should not be all self—though man is.
One should not sink into his own mind away from
his own trouble and another's trouble. There is
another road, Dairne, but it is a road that only a
woman here and there can follow. What said
Clotach, that one man of the reds? 'A green
kirtle on her with open sleeves, and red shoon below
the green, and——' I forget."

"A red belt low on my hips," murmured the
deep, soft voice at his shoulder, "a red selvedge
low on my neck, a silver band in my black hair—
and there is my gold arm-band as well."

"She had her ears open that time," said Flann,
"and, maybe, they are open now, too. But let it
be known that a woman attired in green and red
and silver and gold must be the mover in the game,

not the moved. Dairne has never moved any piece on any board, and gallant raiment would only make itching fingers itch to move her. How can she be like that red-haired woman Alor, my great brother's wife, for whom men killed till the right man came? Or like Maeve of Connacht holding heroes under her thumb with age on her and her children behind her? Can she be like Deirdre, the golden, who broke the sons of Usna and Conchobar the King and all Ulster? Bold and shy, alluring and aloof, the huntress hunted, many things, many things, till her game is played—and she throws the game away. I do not know! I do not know at all! Dairne is listening?"

"Every word I could say again," Dairne spoke lowly.

"Small good that will do her, but I have said my say."

"A long, hard saying," said Dairne, "and a softness running through it like a bird's song."

"Like your own voice, Dairne, that makes my heart sore," half-whispered Flann.

And he was not sure that he caught her whisper.

"Flann of the soft heart."

They went on silently another mile or more until the tracks they were following turned sharply left. There Flann halted and lifted head to look about him. The wide chariot road ran straight ahead into the woods, but there were no tracks on that road; the tracks had turned off into a lane barely wide enough to take a wain or an unscythed chariot. The lane ran up a brief slope and disappeared between two close clumps of furze in full bloom.

"That is the road to the Bruden of Da Derga," said the voice of Dairne.

"Conaire's road—and my road. Fate has not loosed a single mesh."

He set foot on the narrow road, went up the slope, and brushed by a clump of furze. There again he halted to look over the country before him. Open country at last. The woods thinned quickly away to scattered broad oaks in green pastures where dun and black cattle grazed at peace. And beyond the tree-studded green pastures the land lifted itself into smooth curves that swept upward and rolled over and upwards again into brown hills of heather curving and stretching eastwards towards the hidden sea. The whole side of one great hill was a blaze of furze in full bloom, one amazing cloak of red gold on a mighty breast, with the thin pearl haze of spring filming it into fairy loveliness.

"Maur, my brother, would make a song of that, too," said Flann.

He looked over that quiet, sleeping landscape for a long time, and his thoughts troubled him. Once he groaned, as if in pain, and at the end he cried aloud, shaking his head fiercely:

"I do not know! I do not know at all!"

"He cannot make up his mind! It has come to that with him." Dairne's voice lifted at his shoulder.

Flann felt nettled at some small trace of mocking in that remote voice.

"What does Dairne know of the things in my mind?" he asked, derision in his own tone.

"I can follow it, but not when it goes deep into great wisdom or great foolishness."

"Ho-ho! Dairne, the wise woman, who knows the tongue of birds and the thoughts of men! She will now tell me the thing in my mind?"

"Is it an order?"

"Dairne will tell me?"

"This is it. You and the three red robbers are men going before for a man Ingcel with one eye and for Fer Rogain outcast by the King."

"You got that by listening. What is in my mind, Dairne?"

"The plan of Ingcel and Fer Rogain," went on Dairne, "is to wreak a destroying on the Bruden of Da Derga, and you are to lead them to it after making talk of the things and men in the hostel."

"You got that from listening also. The thing in my mind, Dairne?"

"You looked yonder over the rim of the hills where the sea is, and your eyes marched along the hills and stopped at one place, and the thought in your mind was : ' That way they will come and there they will await my coming.' You made one stroke in the dust with the point of your staff, and your thought was : ' To-night they will be waiting for me.' You made a second stroke, and to your thought you added : ' Or the night after this one.' Three times the point of your staff pressed down on the second line, and to yourself you said : ' To-morrow night, to-night, to-morrow night.' And the thought with the words was : ' Conaire the King might stay only the one night at the Bruden, and if I wait until to-morrow night there may be no king to die.' That was the trouble in your mind, Flann of the kind heart, who is vexed with me.''

Flann was silent for a long time, and then he said with extraordinary mildness :

'' Will not Dairne, who is wise, make up my mind for me ? ''

And at once Dairne answered.

'' There is a house I know in the woods near here where we could stay the night and get food. People of good heart, Cailb and her man Snađe, the woodman, and a clann of five, three sons and two daughters, Teiched, Tetscorac and Donn, Blosc and Etin.''

'' It will please them to add two mouths to their seven ? ''

'' They will share what they have.''

'' That is the poor's way, I know,'' said Flann.

He turned round, and his half-shut eyes considered her with an interest that had nothing in it of weariness, and her eyes sank before his.

"We will stay with your woman Cailb and her man Snade," he said slowly, "and their clann of five, whose names I do not remember——"

"Teiched, Tetscorac——"

"You will put your finger on them and name them for me." His slow voice gentled. "I am sorry, Dairne, that I was vexed with you without reason. But I promise you I will be vexed with you often, and often with good reason."

He reached out his left hand and stroked one finger on the soft duskiness of her cheek. The surge of her blood came up to her black hair, and she trembled; and quickly she turned from him and quickly went down the slope to the main road, the black pig trotting at her heels. Flann walked behind the black pig.

## CHAPTER XVIII.

### *Dairne Teaches Flann a Lesson.*

THEY found the woodman's bothy in a small clearing a mile back from the royal road to Naas-na-Righ : a long, low, single-roomed hut of withies roofed with withered rushes. At the sunny side of it was a clay-fenced patch of corn. It was evening then, the sun shining redly among the top branches of the trees, and the thrushes singing.

The clann of children were playing about the door with two half-bred hounds ; the woman-of-the-house was grubbing between the corn ridges with a wooden hoe ; the woodman himself sat on the fence spoke-shaving an unbent bow with a flake of flint.

The half-bred hounds saw them first and hurried with clamour to consume them to the last inch ; and when the hounds saw the bristling small swine the clamour proclaimed the leavings even less than that. But Dairne said carelessly, '' Down, Lum ! Down Sett ! '' And the barking changed its tune to a suspicious welcome, and the hounds circled round Flann to see if he had an ankle worth nipping. But Flann flicked fingers at them, and, dropping their tails, they looked at each other, as much as to say, " These two-legged ones, they will not scare, and the four-footed one, look at his tusks ! Let us go chase a coney." And that they did.

The woodman stayed where he was and went on shaving his bow, but the woman came out of her corn-patch to greet them, two younglings attaching themselves to her skirts and looking round Dairne at Flann. She was a tall, strong, wide, high-breasted woman with black hair, and a face all health and good nature. She looked at Dairne, and looked again, blinking her eyes.

" Indeed and indeed, if it is not Cicuile of Fercal ! "

" I am Dairne now, woman-of-the-house Cailb."

" To be sure ! Your mother's name for you. A blessing on you, and on your pig and on your man."

She embraced Dairne into her great bosom, and took in Flann with her woman's eyes.

" It is good, and better than good, Dairne, my dear, to see you with your beauty on you, and you with a man of your own, and a fine upstanding figure of a man for all his small blemish." She held Dairne away and looked her up and down. " Tell me now—tell me now—— ? "

But Dairne flushing, whispered to her :

" He is one of the great ones from beyond the sea, Flann, son of a prince of swords, going in secret the roads of Erin."

" It could be—it could be ! " She turned her voice towards the man on the fence. " Snade, you gad, here be Dairne that was Cicuile, and her man Flann."

The man slid down off the fence and came slowly, still smoothing the curve of the bow. He was a thin, small, narrow-shouldered man with red-rimmed eyes and hair outrageously red, and all his five half-naked children had hair even redder than his own. He took no notice of Dairne, but came straight at Flann and stood the tall bow in front of him.

" What do you think of that ? "

Flann heeled his staff into the ground, took the tip of the bow in his left hand, swayed it in the air like a fishing rod, looked along the line of it, stood it upright, bent it slowly, unbent it again, and tapped one spot softly with his bronze hook.

" The shaving of your fingernail, and it is a job," said one craftsman to another.

" That is what I think myself," agreed Snade, and resumed his careful shaving. But suddenly he remembered his hostship and let loose an astonishing bellow. " Cailb, you streel, is there nothing to eat in this house and night down on top of us ? "

" Plenty, aplenty," said the big dark woman cheerfully. " Come ye away in, my darlings ! "

A bellied, bronze-riveted pot was bubbling on a low fire of wood embers in the middle of the floor, and a layer of blue wood smoke, eddying lazily four feet above it, made its lazy way through a hole in the roof. The woman emptied the pot into a deep wooden ashet on a low trestle, and there were three rabbits and a couple of kids seething in their own juices, with sopping oaten bannocks around them.

The company sat on hassocks and wooden blocks in a wide circle round the trestle, their heads below the smoke, fingers and teeth busy ; and the young ones scalded their fingers in the hot gravy and sucked them loudly. It was as rich and satisfying a meal as any that Conaire the King might be enjoying in the Hostel of Da Derga.

The children, losing their early shyness, piled round Dairne. They knew Dairne of old. Flann, looking at her, saw a young and generous laughing mother, a child in her lap and a child with soft arms throttling her. One bold lad, Tetscorac, was at Flann's side, his fingers curiously touching the right hand that was a bronze hook. Flann held it up, circled it rapidly, hooked something from the vacant air, looked at it this way and that, and swept off an unseen head with a side chop of his left hand.

" The tenth to-day," said Flann.

He grinned at the lad, and the lad grinned at

him, and was soon busy blowing breath on the
bronze hook and polishing it briskly.

Then the elder girl, Blosc, lifted up her voice.

"Cicuile-Dairne, tell us a story—tell us one of
your lovely stories, Cicuile-Dairne?" And all the
young ones shouted together and apart : "One of
your lovely stories, Cicuile-Dairne?"

Dairne looked shyly at Flann, flushing after her
habit.

"Flann is a great talker," said she. "He will
tell us a story."

"Tell us your lovely story, Cicuile-Dairne!"
Flann ordered sternly.

And Dairne told them a story. This is something like it :

Once upon a time, and a very good time it was,
a mouse and a louse and a red-little-hen lived all
alone and together in a small house under the hill.
And one day the red-little-hen said, "I will bake a
wheaten cake. Who will go out and gather me
five score ears of ripe corn?"

"I will not," said the mouse. "I will not,"
said the louse. "I will do it myself," said the red-
little-hen. And that she did.

"Who, now, will scutch my five score ears of
corn?" said the red-little-hen.

"I will not," said the mouse. "I will not,"
said the louse. "I will do it myself," said the red-
little-hen. And that she did.

" Who, now, will grind my corn in the quern ? "
said the red-little-hen.

" I will not," said the mouse. " I will not,"
said the louse. " I will do it myself," said the red-
little-hen. And that she did.

" Who, now, will knead my fine wheaten
cake ? " said the red-little-hen.

" I will not," said the mouse. " I will not,"
said the louse. " I will do it myself," said the red-
little-hen. And that she did.

" Who, now, will turn my cake on the griddle ?"
said the red-little-hen.

" I will not," said the mouse. " I will not,"
said the louse. " I will do it myself," said the red-
little-hen. And that she did.

And then, and then, the cake was baked, and
the red-little-hen said : " Who, now, will eat my
fine wheaten cake ? "

" I will," said the mouse. " I will," said the
louse. " I will eat it myself," said the red-little-
hen.

" And that she did," shouted the five children,
and Snade and Cailb ; and their laughter made the
smoke eddy. But Flann cried :

" Wait ye ! Wait ye there now ! That is not
the end of that story. That story has a long way
to go yet, and I know the way it went, and it was
this way " :

The mouseen (narrated Flann) was squeaking

tears out of its eyes, and the louse jumping to beat a flea, and the red-little-hen had the cake standing on its edge on the griddle when in walked a man and a woman and a small black pig. Yes, surely! The same and the very same as that small one rooting his nose into the mast out there.

" Ho-ho! Ha-ha! " said the man. " Here is a fine wheaten cake for my dinner." And he made a drive at it like that with his bronze hook.

But behold you! the cake took a jump over the bronze hook. " You will not eat me," cried the cake. A foot high it jumped, and landed on its edge on the middle of the floor, and rolled out the door and down the hill as fast as the wind and twice as handy.

The man and the woman ran after it, leaping and jumping and fly-jumping, but the cake left them standing. But the small black pig was wise as a salmon. He took a short cut and was up with the cake when it came to three women bittling clothes at a well.

" Where are you going, wheaten cake? " asked a washer.

" From a griddle, from a pan—from a woman, from a man—and from you if I can," said the cake, and off it went rolling and doubling and turning somersaults to beat the King's juggler.

And the women threw their bittles after it, but

there was never a woman yet that could hit anything with a bittle but the holes in her man's shirt.

But the little black pig was tough, and he getting his second wind. He took another short cut and was up with the cake, and took a turn out of it like a greyhound, when in it twisted through a barn door where four men were threshing corn.

" Where are you going, wheaten cake ? " asked a thresher.

" From a griddle, from a pan—from a woman, from a man—from three well-washers—and from you if I can."

And off with it out the barn door with a bound and a roll and a leap and a hop. And the men threw their flails after it, but it skipped over them and curled under them, and away. The small black pig held on with might and then with main, gathering the wind of two parishes into its lights, and making two short cuts and a slice off a third, and there he was at a corner ahead of the cake ; and the cake reared up and stopped like a horse at a gate.

" You will kill yourself with the dint of running, my poor wheaten cake," said he, sidling up to it. "Where are you going at all ? "

" From a griddle, from a pan—from a woman, from a man—from three well-washers—from four barn threshers—and from you——"

" G-r-r-r-umph ! " said the small black pig, and

had the cake by one ear, or the twisty bit on the
rim that did for an ear. And over his shoulder he
threw it, and away back with him over hill and over
dale, wood and valley and scarthy places, till he
came to the little house under the hill. And there
was the man and the woman, the mouse, the louse,
and the red-little-hen, and they all thinking they
would be going supperless to bed, the same as
we'll not be going as soon as my mouth is shut in
a short while.

"It is not good to be greedy," said the small
black pig, "and punishment is no cure. Sure,
when all is said and most done, everyone is entitled
to a bite and a sup, and we all decent people."

So he divided the cake into six pieces, and if
some of them were bigger than other pieces, some
of them were smaller, and everyone was happy and
no one spoke a word, for they had good manners
and their mouths full. And that is the end of that
story.

"Did the cake say anything at all?" piped
small Etin.

"Cakes are made to be eaten, small one. It is
their delight. Moreover, no one minded what the
cake said, only the way it tasted, and it a good
way."

"I think I am sorry for the cake," said the girl
sadly. "I will not eat a wheaten cake any more."

And her brothers hooted at her.

"You must make another end to that story, Flann soft-heart," said Dairne, "and set the cake up in the sky like the full moon."

"The end of it will be that her piece of cake gave the woman a pain there is no telling for three days and four nights. Her name was Dairne."

"No-no! Dairne," cried Blosc, smothering Dairne's face with kisses. "He is only teasing you."

"I know that, small darling," whispered Dairne. "And you are young enough to tell him so."

There was clamour by the children for another story, but the mother hushed them.

"Shut-eye time," she said, and went out of the house. She came back with a double-armful of clean straw, and this she spread and shook and smoothed in an empty corner behind the door.

"A poor nest for your man and yourself, Dairne jewel, but the best we can do."

Dairne looked as startled as a roe, but Flann, though startled, had a ready tongue and a laugh with it.

"Woman-of-the-house," said he, "wet and dry I have been sleeping under the sky these three moons. A roof over me is the sod on my grave. I will go and look at the night."

He went out and found the gloaming deepening, but it was no deeper than his thoughts and not half as deep as his cursings. Kindness was frightened in him, for he cursed himself and he cursed Dairne, and the big dark Cailb, and the small red Snade.

"And I would curse the red brats, too," he said, " only they are curse enough already."

But the quiet of the gloaming, in time, silenced him : the desolate even light of it below the trees, the still tracery of young leaves against the pale glow of the north, the darkening hush that went deep and deep into the wood. It was not worth while being angry or afraid, everything was so aloof from anger and from fear.

He went down to the margin of the quick-running stream and under a tall, smooth-boled beech. The high crotch of a root pushed out towards the water, and he sat down at one side of the crotch, his shoulders to the trunk, and his ears listening to the chuckle of the water.

At first he thought the water was laughing softly at him, but as he went on listening he knew that it was laughing its remote laughter at nothing. That was a mad thought. It went on laughing for ever and ever and was laughing at nothing.

There was the stir of a soft foot amongst dry-crumbled beech leaves, and Dairne came down to the brink of the stream. She stood very still, one ear turned to the remote chuckling, and Flann thought that she had not seen him. He spoke softly.

"Dairne was too proud to stay alone in her bed of straw?"

Dairne did not answer him.

"One woman would not let another woman know."

Dairne went on listening to the water.

"What is the stream saying, Dairne of the tongues?"

"It is only part of a tongue," murmured Dairne, "like the wind, like the tide, like the stir at the roots of grass. Often and often I nearly had it, but I was afraid. No, I do not know that tongue—I dare not—but I know what the birds are whispering above your head."

"I do not hear them, but tell me?"

She took a small step towards him, but hesitated.

"Sit down here and tell me. You are not afraid?"

Dairne sat down at the other side of the crotch, almost near enough for her shoulder to touch his. He threw a corner of his cloak over her.

"I know what fear is, but to-night I am not afraid at all." Soft and low the murmur of her voice.

"There will be other nights," said Flann deeply. "What do the birds whisper?"

"There is a clann of ten—I think ten—gold finches on one branch, waiting to take their turn on the nests lined with feathers over there in the furze. They are grumbling about that and about us. There is a red linnet on her nest and her mate on a twig ; there is a thrush on a high bough thinking of a new song to make the sun rise, and a blackbird top of all, but the blackbird sings only three notes when Beltane is at hand. As I came across the grass a finch said : ' This two-legged will not throw a stick at us like the small red ones that run and hide.' ' I would not put it past her,' said another, and the linnet said, ' I saw her mate with a stick.' And the thrush said, ' They will sleep, and I will wake them with a song at dawn.' The blackbird said nothing.''

'' Whether that came out of your head or your hearing,'' said Flann, ''it sounds like the truth, and, maybe, we should sleep as the thrush said.''

He went into a muse of his own. She was not afraid, and that was no compliment to a man, unless—but no use thinking about that. He was afraid. He felt something—something that was not new and that he thought was dead—stirring inside him. He did not like it. This shy, wild, wise thing of the woods was here under his hand ; he had only to put his hand out to touch her. A shy, wild thing and unafraid of him, and he could break her and go the road careless of her and her brokenness. A thought like that was an ugly thing. It kept coming back when he was not watching. Let her remain wild and shy as long as she could.

She was doomed at the end of the road, but let him not be the end of that road. . . . He would fold his arms under his cloak. A man could sit with folded arms, and by some inertia of will keep his arms folded—keep them folded—keep them folded so . . .

He was standing on the left of the slope below his father's long house at Baravais. It was the dawn of a summer morning, and the sun had touched to rose the peaks of The Ser. His father, Orugh, squat and strong and old, came out under the lintel and yawned, and laid his hands on the rail in front of the door. "You are welcome home, Flann," he said, and welcome was in his eyes, and Flann had a new happiness to see the welcome there. Maur, his young brother, came to his father's side, his supple, strong brown body naked to the waist, and a wooden whistle in his hand. He smiled at Flann and put the whistle to his lips, but no sound came. To the right of his father's house was Delgaun's house that he had helped Delgaun to build. Through the open door he could see red-haired Alor busy about a new fire, and he liked Alor but did not love her any longer. Delgaun, that steadfast man that had been the terrible Stone-Face, sat in his armed chair, his son upon his knees, and his deep, quiet voice spoke. "You will need more this morning, Alor. Flann is coming home. I saw him on the road, and knew how much I missed him." "He will spoil my son more than you," said Alor, a pot in her hand, "but I am glad, too." And Flann was happier than before. To the left of his father's house was another house—a new fine house—and Flann wondered at it. "That is the place for my house," said Flann. "Who dared build that house there?" The door of the house was open, but there was a strange darkness inside it. He looked into the darkness and listened. There was a stir in there and then a child softly whimpered, and Flann's flesh stirred. Again the child whimpered, and out of the darkness came a soft, wordless, lulling croon, and again Flann's flesh stirred. "That house is mine," said Flann. "I will see who whimpers and who croons." He was about to stride forward when Maur's whistle began to play, and the playing tied his feet to the ground. He could not move though he summoned all his numb will to his aid. "Stop playing, brother," he cried. "I must see." And Maur stopped playing to say: "It is forbidden. It is not the time. Turn round and go away and come again." And sadly he turned away, and slowly went down the slope, and the lift and run and tripple of Maur's whistle was all about him like a bird singing. . . .

That was the thrush's song that awaked Dairne at the first streak of dawn. She waked quietly and completely like all wild things, and slowly turned her head to look at Flann. He was sound asleep, his head back against the trunk and his shoulder almost touching hers. She moved softly and her shoulder did touch his. Then she slipped aside from under her share of the cloak and rose to her feet, one of which was still asleep. She stood tapping her tingling foot softly on the ground, and looked down at Flann's tilted face. It was calm as death. Even the nostrils did not move with his breathing. A long, sternly sad face, no longer ironic, with a clear brow and firm mouth, and strong bones under the skin—the face of a man ! Then he sighed deeply, and Dairne, putting a hand to her mouth, turned and slipped away amongst the trees by the course of the stream.

The small black swine came trotting briskly out of the wood, and there was brown mould on its snout and adrift on its shoulders. He grunted softly and nuzzled the back of her knee, and Dairne rubbed behind his ears before tweaking one of them.

" Go and finish your meal, dirty one ! " she ordered. And the dirty one trotted back to his scuffling in the beech mast.

She went up through the wood till, in a curve within a copse of sallagh, she found a pool deep enough to take her above her knees. There she soaked and bathed herself from the crown of her head to the soles of her feet, using the fine gravel for a cleanser as Flann had done. She came out to squeeze the water out of her curls and race up and and down the bank to dry herself, tossing her hair and holding her voice from singing. She wanted to sing and shout but she dared not. She put the song in her flying feet and the throw of her arms. When she was nearly dry she slipped her red gold band above her elbow and stood admiring it, turning her arm this way and that to make curves that were curves. As she stood thus it might be worth limning her as she was limned in a writing that is ten centuries old.

" Dark and shining as the back of a stag-beetle her hair and her eyebrows. A shower of pearls her teeth, browner than hazelnut her eyes, red as rowan berries her lips. Smooth and soft—whiter than snow—her shoulders. White as the foam of the wave the flank, slender, long, tender, smooth, soft as wool. Polished and warm, sleek and white the two thighs ; short and rule-straight the two shins ; justly arched the two feet. The radiance of the moon in her face, the loftiness of pride in her smooth eyebrows, the light of wooing in her eyes. A dimple in each of her cheeks, with a dappling of red in the bright lustre of snow. Of the world's women she was the dearest and loveliest and justest that the eyes of man had ever beheld."

But whatever eyes beheld her the eyes of Flann did not, for, when she got back to the beech tree, Flann was still asleep, slumped down under his cloak, and his head drifting sideways on the smooth bole. The sun was not yet risen though the east was red, and Flann's face looked pinched and wan in the cold light. Very carefully Dairne slipped into her place under the cloak, and very carefully brought Flann's drifting head down on her shoulder. He sighed softly but did not wake, and there was a tenderness woeful in its beauty about Dairne's mouth.

An hour later Flann awaked. He, too, waked quietly, opening his eyes and remaining still. Dairne's neck was close to his eyes, white as curd, soft as wool, warm with life ; and a small pulse beat and beat through the pearl glow of it. He could smell the dusky scent of her hair. He could set his teeth in the small pulse and bite it through. He could do many things. He lay still and did nothing. In time he lifted his head slowly, slowly moved sideways from below the cloak, and rose to his feet.

He stood looking down at Dairne, his hand lax but his mouth firm. She seemed sound asleep. The black, not quite dry hair, curled on her white brow, her eyelids above black lashes were faintly tinged with blue, young blood was in her cheeks, her nose, that was of no particular shape, gave a small, wistful, half-animal twitch, and her mouth— her mouth was so tender and soft and gentle and generous, that he was urgent to bend down and kiss it with a gentleness that might grow to ardour.

But that thing, too, he did not do. Instead he bent and moved the corner of the cloak over her bare feet, took his staff from the ground, and, step by step, moved backwards and aside, till Dairne was hidden by the trunk of the tree. Then he turned on his heel and ran and ran and ran.

Dairne's eyes were open and she heard him run. But she made no move to follow. She stayed where she was under his cloak until the sound of his running feet had died down in the distance. Then she got up and went through the wood, Flann's cloak on her arm, and the small black swine following after. Her practised eye saw the faint toemarks, the snapped twig, the swaying briar, the broken gossamer, the tracks in the dew across open places. They led her to the royal road where the long-paced footmarks were easily followed in the dust that carried minute specks of dew. Still she followed, back along the road she had come before, till she came to the narrow track that turned to the Bruden of Da Derga. Farther she did not go.

She stopped there, her head down, her feet still, her whole body still, all the life in her sunk inwards to a final contemplation. Here, now, was her destiny staring her in the face. Here, at the fork of this road, she must decide for good or ill, for good and ill, which road she must take. And there would be no turning back.

At the end she drew in a deep breath that was not a sigh, drew Flann's old brown cloak about her as if it were a mantle of coloured silk, and went back through the trees to the woodman's hut. The black pig grunted with some disgust, but followed after.

Cailb, the dark woman, was busy with a pot at the fire; the children tumbled on the floor or sat still eyeing the pot; Snade had gone out to try his new bow.

"Woman-of-the-house," said Dairne, "Flann, my man, has gone to the Bruden of Da Derga."

"There was enough for ye both, and both welcome."

"He has a high business of his own that called him. Yesterday he told me the thing I am to do. It is a hard thing, but I must do it for his sake and mine. Will you lend me your shears and your needle, and give me two threads of your sewing hank?"

"And my hands as well," said the kindly woman, "and a bit of a green ribbon."

## CHAPTER XIX.

### *The Hostel of Da Derga.*

EVEN-TIDE, with the sun shining orange over the high-pitched, rye-thatched roof of the hostel, and all the company beginning the evening meal in the inner courtyard. The wall of the hostel, with its seven inner carved doorways, entirely circled the paved courtyard, and the Dothra River, running over clean gravel, cut it in two between terraced banks of stone. A wooden bridge without rails joined the two parts.

On a wide stone platform above the water three fires of wood and charcoal were burning redly, and on the fires three immense pots steamed, and a multitude of small pots bubbled. Cooks and menials moved about the pots, and the cooks, after their habit, were as red as the fire in face and tongue.

Conaire the King and the leading men of his company—Conall Cernach, MacEcht, Cormac Condlongas and Cuscrad of Ulster, the three blond princes of East Britain, and many others—sat about a long narrow bench in their own half of the

courtyard, attendants about them ; and the host,
Da Derga, portly, red-haired, red-bearded, wearing a green robe with a white hood, overlooked the
serving, and saw that the methers, the piggins, the
silver-bound horns were never empty of mead or
wine or uisgebaugh.

The rest of the company sat where they pleased
and how they pleased : on the stone terrace, against
the wall, on the edge of the pillared platform around
the circle of the house ; and when anyone wanted
his platter filled he took it himself to the cooking
fires, and the cooks filled it from this pot and that
without consulting tastes. There was no woman in
the company that evening, but, notwithstanding,
there was a babel of talk that drowned the babble
of the Dothra. The pipers and harpers were not
yet playing.

Apart from the others, in the angle made by the
river and the wall, four men sat side by side on the
edge of the platform. They were not so much apart
as drawn away from. The rest of the company
looked crookedly at them with sullenness and a little
fear, and if the hostel had not been Da Derga's,
with the High King for guest, the fear might have
led to worse than crooked looks. Three of the men
had laid aside red cloaks, red shields, red helmets,
but they were still as red as ever. The fourth man
had no cloak either, and his leather-belted saffron
tunic showed his bare sinewy neck and bare sinewy

brown arms. For right hand he had a bronze hook.

On the ground before the four was a beechen basin full of meats, and a hooped piggin crowned with cream froth, and the four were busy eating, and drinking in turn.

" Flann, my brother," said Clotach, " the night will soon be here ? "

" It will be here without you telling me," said Flann sourly.

" Maybe I should not remind you," said Clotach equably, " but there is a small journey before you."

" And before ye three."

" Do not let us say anything about that," said Clotach. " Look ! why does that guard hurry ? "

One of the outer door-wards was hurrying across the wooden bridge to where Da Derga stood behind the King's shoulder. He whispered in his master's ear, and Da Derga turned with him and, frowning, crossed the bridge and went into the house. He was back in two minutes, went directly to the King, and whispered in his ear. The King in turn frowned, and his hand sought the curls of his red young beard. Then he said aloud :

" I will speak with her, whoever she is."

He went out, Da Derga behind him, and all the company that had heard looked at his back with troubled eyes.

The King found a woman at the outer doorway.

She stood still and straight and dark against the wheel of a chariot, the westering sun shining red about her. A long brown cloak fell to her heels. In one hand she held the end of a straw rope, and the other end of it was tied to the foreleg of a shapely black swine showing the beginning of its fighting tusks. She did not look at the King, but down the length of the passage behind him to where the cooking fires glowed in the courtyard.

The King did not look at her either. He looked at the swine.

"I have seen you before," he said. He lifted eyes to the woman who was not looking at him. "And you, too, I think. Woman, what do you see?"

"Light shining through the door, and another geasa broken by the High King."

"Not much of a geasa," said the King dryly. "Is that all you see?"

"I see birds bearing flesh in their claws," she answered him in a low, deep voice.

"All who augur, augur ill for me," he said harshly, "but good only comes. What is your name?"

Her eyes met his then and met them boldly. Bold brown eyes drooping insolently below black brows! No one could know how hard her heart beat.

"I was Cicuile and now I am Dairne."

"One or the other is not much of a name."

"If I lose what I seek I will be known by many names."

"And what names are they?"

"Easy to say, O King: Samon, Sinand, Seisclend, Soab, Sanlocht, Caill, Dichoem, Dichuil, Dithim, Dichuimne, Dichruidre, Egem, Agam, Ethamne, Grinn, Cluiche, Cethardam, Nith, Nemain, Neonnen, Badb, Bloar, Huae, Oe Aife la Struth, Mache, Mede, and Mod."

Leaning on one foot, holding up one hand, breathing one breath, she half-chanted all these ancient ominous names in the King's face. He nodded.

"I know that wicked litany," he said, "and the nameless stories about it and them. I swear by the gods I adore that I will never call you by any of them. What is it that you desire?"

"That which you desire, but now only meat in my mouth and a bed to lie on."

The King looked out at the west. The last tip of the sun was sinking beyond the plain that spread immensely westwards beyond and below the mouth of the valley that the hostel spanned.

"You speak of geasas. It is a geasa of mine not to receive the company of one woman after sunset, and it is the one geasa that I would keep." He smiled grimly. "It has saved me much trouble in many houses I have slept in."

"It is your geasa, O King. But I have no geasas."

"If it is a toll you seek I will give you the mate of that black one and food off my table if you stay outside the seven doorways this night."

Dairne lifted up her head, contempt in her hooded eyes.

"The High King of Erin denies a meal and a bed to a lone woman! Is the generosity of this house withered?"

"That is a hard saying," said the King, and looked at Da Derga.

Da Derga moved his red head weightily.

"It is my geasa not to close six doors, but for you, Conaire, my lord, I will——"

"It is a good geasa, yours, my friend," said the King, "and my foolish one can go with the others. Let the woman enter."

He turned and went back to his company, and Da Derga, saying no word to the woman, followed after.

The door-ward drew up against the wall to avoid the touch of this woman of ill omen, and Dairne walked down the passage and out on the platform above the courtyard, where the light of evening was still strong. She stood there looking over all the company, her head up and her eyes looking under black lashes; and a murmur rose from the court-yard, and deepened to a growl, and died away.

But Dairne took no least notice. She threw her brown cloak back from her shoulders so that it swept behind her, stepped down on the pavement and walked slowly, smoothly towards the angle made by wall and river. And the black pig walked at her side.

She was tall, and nobly tall. A green ribbon hemmed the bleached smock that came down to the middle of her straight shins; a green ribbon was belted low on her hips; the smock had been new-shaped to her young breasts, and the low, square-cut collar was selvedged with green and showed throat and neck like the swell of an ivory column. Her arms were bare to the shoulder, white as milk, curved like an eastern blade, and the right one carried a twisted clasp of gold above the elbow. Her eyes glowed dark and sombre between black lashes, two spots, red as foxglove, were on her cheeks, her red, unsmiling mouth held passion and promise on tight rein. Over one ear a yellow daffodil was set in her black curls. And her heart beat hard against her side, but only herself knew that.

"By the fingerbones on which my tribe swears!" cried Clotach. "It is Dairne that was Cicuile. What her name is now would make a man wonder!"

Flann gave her one quick, clear glance and no more. He turned and sat staring in front of him, the lines of his face stern and deeply carved. But Conal's welcome was warm enough for all. He hurriedly opened a space between himself and Flann, and patted it with his hand.

"Dairne, my darling! Sit down here and be fed."

She did not deign to reply. She tied the straw rope to a pillar standing out of the platform, and then came and sat down between Flann and Conal. To Flann she turned.

"Flann one-hand, there is your black pig, and this is your cloak. You left them behind."

Flann made no movement and no word. But Clotach at his other side laughed.

"One excuse is as good as another," said he, "and that cuts with two edges."

"I am not sure how right you are, Clotach," said Dairne.

Conal picked up the beechen basin, looked at the broken meats, emptied them into the river, and stalked across to the cooking pots. He brought the basin back steaming, and held it under Dairne's nose.

"A pullet out of its first feathers!" he coaxed her.

She stripped off a wing and side of a breast and ate it carefully, slowly; then broke off the other wing and picked it daintily.

" Do not let it be walking on its two legs," urged Conal.

She moved the basin aside, and he laid it hastily down to pick up the piggin of ale. She moved that aside, too, rose to her feet, went down the steps to the river, rinsed her hands and her mouth, and, cupping her hands, drank neatly. She waved her hands to dry them in curves that drew the eye, and the gold band gleamed in the white light of the gloaming. Then she came up the steps and took her place close to Flann.

Conal, the doomed moth, took his seat close to her. He was scorched but not blind yet, for his eye moved from her white arms to the ivory column of her neck swelling to her young bosom, and in his eyes were something of awe and daring.

" To be sure ! " said he. " Here is something to match your band of gold."

He took his gold-and-bronze brooch from his shoulder and pinned it with slow care on the green selvedge below her throat, his head close as he dared ; and calmly she let him do it, not even looking at him.

" There ! " said Conal with satisfaction, and slipped an arm cautiously round her beneath the cloak.

" Your manners, red Conal the robber ! " she warned him coldly, and shook his arm away.

" That is right," said Conal agreeably. " One

should not be too easy." And forthwith took a firmer grip of her.

And, forthwith, he got his due and a little more.

"Flann gave me a lesson yesterday," she said quietly, "and you will get your share of it now, Conal."

And with the full length of her arm, and with her firm hand clenched, and with all the might that was in her, she hit him behind the ear. He yelped like a puppy and fell forward off the platform on his hands and knees, his eyes shut and his head wagging sideways to ease the sting. And Clotach, laughing hugely, picked up the wooden piggin and brought it plashing and solid on the back of his head. Conal flattened out on the stones, lay still while one might count ten, stirred, came to his hands, resumed his head shaking, and sat back on his heels. He looked at Flann with dazed eyes.

"What did she hit me with?"

"With her fist."

Conal felt the back of his head.

"Her fist? There is a hollow to hold an apple, and my blood running down my backbone. Her fist?"

"It was a hard fist," said the choking Clotach.

Conal looked at his wet hand, blinked and looked again. There was no blood on it.

"Your blood has turned to sour ale, my poor fellow," Clotach told him.

237

Conal grinned sheepishly and rose to unsteady feet.

"I was near making a mistake that time," he said, looked at the utterly calm Dairne out of the side of an eye, and went and sat down at the other end of the row by his laughing brother, Cetach.

Cetach wiped his eyes and drew in his breath.

"I was watching him," he said delightedly. "I saw him leading up to it, and he with no more understanding than the chicken with its two legs. And his fine brooch gone, too." Again he started to roar.

"Wait till my head stops going round," Conal threatened, "and it is yourself will laugh crooked."

"That is enough now," ordered Clotach the leader. "Take you your lesson, brother!"

"Whatever you say, Clotach." Conal was agreeable.

The two red brothers had made the courtyard ring with their laughter, and even Flann had smiled, but they were the only men there who had made merry. The rest of the company looked with distrust and gloom on these ominous guests making brutal horseplay in the presence of the King.

"I was thinking of your lesson all this day, Flann," said Dairne turning to him.

"That last was in no lesson of mine," said Flann coldly, not turning to her. "You will find that out if you play some man with the strong arm."

"The only lesson for Conal!" said Dairne easily. "There is no harm in him—as there would be in Clotach and in you. And I would have a lesson for ye, too."

"All lessons may end here before the dawn," said Flann remotely.

"And a good end it may be." Her voice vibrated. "A good end for Dairne! To end here and be done—done—done! To have no fear any more—and no desire."

"I do not know! I do not know at all!" said Flann.

"The thing you say often." She placed her hand on his wrist above the bronze hook, but her cool fingers did not press. "Do not grieve for me, Flann. This is good. This gives me happiness. I am glad to be here where my end will be clean. It is good."

Flann looked down at her hand, the lines deep about his mouth. Then he quietly drew his arm away and looked about the courtyard. The courtyard was emptying. The King and his company had gone into the house. Lights came out here and there through carved window openings.

"Our roads part here, Dairne," said Flann, and rose to his feet.

"I know that. This is the end. I will not follow you again." Her voice was low and as even as his own.

Flann did not look at her. He walked down the platform to the open doorway through which the King had gone, and there he turned head.

"I am ready, Clotach."

Clotach gestured to his brothers not to move, and went to where Flann stood in the doorway.

"Has the hour come, Flann?"

"The same as any other hour. I am waiting for you."

"You must go?" Clotach whispered.

"Unless you hold me, and you are stronger."

"I will not do that. Your word binds you."

"No word binds me."

"That is between Ingcel and you. Listen now! A path runs up by the course of the Dothra in the hollow of the valley. Follow that. You cannot go wrong. Two miles up a stream comes in on the side of that—your good hand. Turn with it and round the first corner, and there you are. That is the Hollow-of-the-Thrushes, where Fer Rogain waits you."

"And you, too." Flann looked at him through the dying light. "Are ye not coming?"

"We stay here."

"There is your word to Fer Rogain?" Flann reminded him.

"I am keeping it. I led you to the Hostel, and with my tongue I lead you to the Hollow-of-the-Thrushes. After that I stay by my King."

" You will die here ? "

" Others will die as well—and Dairne." He caught Flann's arm. " Take the woman, Flann."

" I do not play that game any more, Clotach," he said sternly, shaking away the hand. " She is safer here than with Tulchinne of the Rapine."

" Who will be here ? I know what is in your mind, brother." He placed a hand on his own breast and then on Flann's. " When the end comes I will make her end clean—if that is the only way."

" You are the man, Clotach."

" There are worse names on me," said Clotach. " You are going now."

Flann went into the house without another word. In time he came to the ward of one of the doors.

" Do you go out ? " the man challenged surlily.

" Is there a rule ? "

" No rule."

" I will be back."

" Had I my way," said the guard, " you would not go far and you would not be back."

" A man like you is not given his own way," Flann told him with contempt and went out.

He went round a chariot with its pole pointing to the sky, and walked out into the gloaming that was now deepening into night. He did not walk far, but stopped by the side of a furze bush on the edge of the track above the stream, and looked up the valley. The hills folded down in two great breasts, grey-purple against the southern blue where a star was shining. Between the breasts his road lay, and at the end of the road were iron men waiting for him to say the word that would bring them down like wolves to the slaughter.

"I do not know! I do not know at all!" said Flann.

"I will know for you, one-hand," said a whisper that came up from the ground and was in his ear. By the side of the furze rose a tall figure, and a strong arm was across Flann's back.

"I know myself now, Ingcel the destroyer," said Flann. "You make it easy for me. And I the first of the dead."

"You were long in coming," said Ingcel, ignoring that. "I came down to look for you, and I was lying here watching the fire through the chariot wheels, wondering how dead you were—or how false?"

"Give me my chance over again and see how false I can be," said Flann, and turned to look back at the hostel. A glow came through an open door and the spokes of the chariot wheel stood out against it. There was another of Conaire's geasas broken.

"Where are the three red ones?" Ingcel still held Flann.

"They are in there."

"Traitors?"

" No. Their mouths are shut. Clotach is no traitor, but Conaire is his King."

" Conaire ? "

" He is there. Conaire, the High King of Erin ! "

Flann felt Ingcel's hand tighten and his breast lift with a long breath.

" It is just." His voice was unmoved. " Fate plays this game fairly."

" Heed me, Ingcel one-eye ! " pleaded Flann. " That house is a fit one for your destruction, but if you have any ruth left, you, a king, will not wreak destruction on the noble king that rests in it to-night."

Ingcel considered that.

" I am getting old, it must be," he murmured then. " Your words touch me. But "—his voice hardened—" to be Prince of Cumbria and King of the Picts, a man must have no ruth, once the first blood is spilled. I remember whose the blood was."

A voice lifted behind them from one of the doorways of the hostel.

" Who growls there ? Begone hounds ! "

Something whizzed over their heads, and Ingcel pulled Flann to his knees. " Down ! A thrown spear ! " he whispered. " Come ! The rest must be said before the leading men."

## CHAPTER XX.

### *Flann Makes His Plea.*

IN a circus-shaped hollow secluded from the main valley, and not more than two miles above the Bruden, Ingcel and Flann stood before a camp fire beginning to burn down, and looked across it at a sitting half-circle of the leading men : Tulchinne the Pict, the sons of Donn Dessa, young Eiccel close to Fer Rogain, many others. Close behind the leaders, on the steep curving side of the hollow, the whole body of reivers crouched in orderly lines one above the other. Now and again, a small flame flickered and hissed and gleamed for a moment on bronze and iron, and brought out the angles of fierce, strongly-moulded faces. Every man was equipped to take the road, and each man held a stone in his right hand.

Fer Rogain looked up at Ingcel.

'' How is it, Prince ? ''

Ingcel, lifting up his voice for all to hear, answered him directly.

'' The Bruden of Da Derga as it stands, with

whatever is in it and whoever is in it, I accept as my right and my full due out of the hands of Fer Rogain."

"Well may you accept it, O Ingcel! It is all yours."

Mad Lomna Druth tossed up his head and his hair, and his mad eyes glistened in the fire-flicker.

"Brother, brother! Do not promise all."

"It is promised," said Fer Rogain, and Fer Gair and Fer Le echoed him.

But Tulchinne the Pict, driven by some inner jealousy and inner greed, lifted up his broad hand.

"We would hear what the house holds. The decision is with us as much as Ingcel."

Ingcel looked down at him narrow-eyed.

"I will let you open your mouth a little longer, Tulchinne," he said. "Flann one-hand will tell you what he has seen."

"Speak on, one-hand," ordered Tulchinne.

Flann looked about the ring slowly. For a draw of breath he was minded to keep his mouth shut and let the decision stand with Ingcel, but then some faint final hope stirred in him, and he lifted up his chin. The moment was his.

"I will speak what I have seen, and whom, within the seven doorways of that hostful kingly house. It is a house of great wealth. It is wealthier than Ormlyth that ye sacked; it is wealthier than the Dun of Ingcel that some of ye would sack; it is wealthier than the two of them together; it is wealthier than any house I have seen or heard of this side of great Rome."

A pleased lifting murmur filled the hollow, and Tulchinne cried out:

"That is the house for me."

"Precious silks and hangings," went on Flann, "gold and silver and bronze, jewels and ivory, shields and swords wrought in gems, ornaments for breast and head and arm, tooled leather for foot and thigh, horns and methers scrolled in gold, vestments and robes for princes and the women of princes, ye will fill the long ships gunwale deep—if ye live to see the sea again."

"Live?" cried Tulchinne. "Is the house held?"

"The house is held. This night the house is full."

A fire of angry, eager questions went round the rings.

"They know we are here? Who is the spy? Where are the red hounds? How many? Who holds it?"

Flann raised his hand and his voice, glad that he had stirred doubt in them.

"There are in the house to-night one hundred, half a hundred, ten and one—and one woman."

"I will look at her," said Tulchinne of the Rapine. "Let her wait." He flung his hand towards the lines of men on the slope. "There are eight hundreds here. I saw them fight at Ormlyth. They fight. Are your three fifties, ten and one, all fighters?"

"They will fight. Half of them are hard-trained in fight, and some of them are of the greatest in the world."

Tulchinne laughed mockingly. "I have killed the greatest in the world, and it is a strange thing that they will not stay dead."

"There is a cause and a leader to-night worth a thousand of ten hundreds."

"Good indeed!" cried Tulchinne the fearless. "Spoil after spilt blood is the only spoil worth the gathering."

Lomna Druth, the mad one, tossed his live lint hair.

"Do not mock us, one-hand," he cried shrilly. "Tell us who is in the house?"

"You know, mad one," said Flann, "but you will listen to me telling my own way. First there is Da Derga, that noble red host, and under him his house-steward, and under the house-steward six door-wards, six swineherds, six horseboys, six table servants, six cup-bearers, six kitcheners, and six cooks."

"Underlings all," said Tulchinne with contempt.

"Da Derga goes about keeping an eye on all things, eating a bite with this one, drinking a mether with that one, listening to the other one's joke that he has heard before, and his laughter ready. Under his orders are one fosterling, three brehons, three poets, nine harpers, nine pipers, three jugglers, three conjurers, three lampooners, and three mimes."

Lomna Druth held up a thumb and four fingers.

"One man, and fourscore without a name."

"If there is a fighting hero amongst them put a name to him, one-hand," taunted Tulchinne.

"And yet, black fool, life is more precious to them than to a hero or to a Pict, and more useful."

"It will be a short life now," said Tulchinne, "and a short life for you, too, one-hand, if you are not careful."

"Someone will need to be careful," said Ingcel softly.

"There are fourscore left, slow-mouth," cried Lomna Druth.

"Count you them. Five head-charioteers, five under-charioteers, three pole men, twelve men of the fore-guard, and twelve men of the rear-guard."

"These will fight," admitted Tulchinne.

"Who leads them, who leads them?" That was Lomna Druth.

"They are led. There are three short dark men of Mercia, three dark tall men of Dalcas, three blonde men of East Britain, three squat men of the Picts, three brown tall Fomorians, three giants of Falga, and three red men of Cualla."

"The throats of these three traitors I will cut with my own hand," roared Tulchinne.

"If you meet one of them," said Flann, "you will know it—for a little while."

"You are coming to it now, one-hand. Oh woe—woe—woe!" cried Lomna Druth.

"Listen then. Before coming out of the hostel to-night I went down the passage where the great rooms are, and into each room I looked. In one wide high room there were two chiefs and twelve companions. One of the chiefs was tall, golden-haired, beardless, with a face wide above, narrow below. He carried a javelin with five barbs, and his shield had five golden circles. The other chief was a stripling with black hair, and he spoke with a stammer."

Fer Rogain stiffened from the hips and fear grew in his eyes.

"I know them," he said, and fear was in his voice. "They are the great Cormac Condlongas, son of Concobhar of Ulster, and his half-brother, Cuscrad Menn. They have never slain men on account of their misery nor spared men because of their wealth." He lowered his voice. "They were hostages with Conaire at Tara."

"You have named them," said Flann, and went on: "I looked into another room, and there was in it a huge warrior and three of his pupils. He was black from head to heel, and his bush of beard was the blackest of him. His shield was black, his axe black, and black the spear that would not stand upright in the height of the room. You know him, Fer Rogain?"

Fer Rogain's head was on his breast now, and his lax hands rested over his knees. He was like a man waiting patiently for the final blow.

"Easy to liken that man," he said dully. "That is MacEcht, the son of Snaide Techid, the battle soldier of Conaire. He shears heads, and scatters brains, and strews entrails."

"That is his name, whatever he does," said Flann. "I looked into a third room. There was but one man in it. A tall, lean, supple panther, with curled blonde-red hair, and a blood-red oblong shield riveted with gold. One cheek was as white as snow, one red as foxglove, one eye blue as hyacinth, one black as a beetle. Liken thou him, Fer Rogain?"

"Easy for me to liken that man with the plashed cheek, and his red shield, Bricriu. The men of Erin, and Alba, and Britain know him. Since the raven perched on Cuchulain's shoulder he is the best hero behind a shield in the land of Erin. He is the great Conall Cernach, son of Amorgen of the Red Branch of Ulster. He slays quickly. He was on a visit of honour to Conaire at Tara."

"You know him. I went into another room, a small room opening from the largest, most splendid room of the hostel. On a low couch a boy slept and dreamed, and as he dreamed he wept. A youth of ten springs, his face freckled with the sun's kiss, and his hair three colours under the sun's ardour. You do not know him, Fer Rogain?"

Fer Rogain shook his heavy head.

"It could not be," he murmured hopelessly. "Surely it cannot be. That youth could not be my little Le Fri Flait. Le Fri Flait never leaves his father's side, and his father Conaire is at Tara."

"You have named him," said Flann without pity, and Fer Rogain's shoulders shook.

"I looked into the large room curtained in silver," went on Flann. "Two youths sat on the side of a great couch, and they played softly on golden pipes. On the couch a lord lay sleeping. A young man still, with a noble white brow and a soft, red-curled beard, and a gold band in his red-curled hair. The mantle over his feet, of the sheen of a peacock's plume, had a golden wheel on one shoulder, and a white bird brown-speckled on the other. He slept, and, as he slept a hound howled, and he awoke out of his sleep and sat upright. 'I heard my hound, Ossar, howl!' He spoke, and looked with troubled, stern blue eyes at his two pages. 'I heard Ossar howl out of an evil dream.' 'Sleep, beloved one,' they comforted him, and went on playing softly on their golden pipes. But their beloved one chanted lowly to the run of the music :

' The howl of Ossar in dream so evil,
The peal of war in Derga's Hostel,
Cold wind of fear from perilous water,
Red feast of swords in the sack of Tara,
Cornfields waste where chariots totter,
Lament of death o'ercoming laughter,
The death of kings where grey wolves prowl,
That I heard in Ossar's howl.'

"That noble man who chanted lay down again, closing his stern, sad eyes, and the golden pipes went on softly playing." Flann lifted his voice savagely. "Name you that man, son of Donn Dessa. I am done. Name you him, and, if Ingcel one-eye has no pity, there is your mad oath to be broken, and four hundred men to do your killing in this hollow. I am done."

A deep, blood-ready growl grated from the hill-side where the men of Erin crouched. Tulchinne, silent at last, moved aside from Fer Gair who was shaking, and fear was in the Pict for the first time. But Ingcel stood still as that rock that watched over Cumbria.

Fer Rogain rose slowly to his feet and faced Ingcel across the camp fire. All the blood was drained out of his face, and the bones of his face stood out under the drawn skin. He began to speak very quietly and very slowly, but as he went on his voice gathered intensity.

"The end is come, then, and I the bringer of that end. I was at the beginning of the road, and I am at the end of it now, and I made the road. All doom was in this game we played, and where the great game is played kings die. Easy for me to name that man, O Ingcel. He is Conaire the Great, son of Eterscel, the High King of Erin. He is my foster-brother that suckled the same breast. He is the most splendid and noble and beautiful and mighty King that has come into the whole world. He is the mildest and gentlest and most perfect. In him there is no blemish in form or shape or carriage, in eye or hair or brightness, in wisdom or skill or eloquence, in splendour or abundance or dignity, in knowledge or valour or mercy. He is Conaire."

A woeful hopeless appeal was in his voice now.

"Good is his reign, O Ingcel! You made peace in Cumbria, so did he make peace in Tara—till in a mad play I broke it. Until I broke that peace no cloud hid the sun from spring to autumn, no dewdrop fell from the grass till height of sun, no wind stirred a beast's tail, no wolf attacked the flocks save the two beasts of Carna, no voice was raised in anger, no rapine wrought, no sword drawn against the law in Erin. In his reign there were four crowns : the crown on his own head, the crown of corn ears, the crown of flowers, and the crown of oak mast. That is the man we would crown with death to-night, O Ingcel! I, too, am done."

Young Eiccel leaped to his feet and threw an arm across Fer Rogain's shoulder.

" Know mercy, my brother! " he cried at Ingcel. " You cannot destroy that noble King."

Nothing moved in Ingcel but his voice, and his voice was stern as death.

" Can we move a step aside from the road you made, Fer Rogain, from the road that I set foot on with you on the shoulders of the sea? An oath was taken, a lot cast, a sword drawn, and my father, the King of Britain, and his seven sons died under your swords in the destruction that I gave you. Will you deny me mine now? Has the time come to sheath the sword? Say it."

Fer Rogain's chin struck his breast and his arms went lax. Ingcel would not let him go.

" Say it! " he challenged. " The choice is yours. Is it time to sheath the sword? "

" It is not time." Fer Rogain threw back his head, and the words were torn out of him.

Lomna Druth was raving on his feet, his eyes alive with madness, and life in his lint hair.

" Fool—fool—fool! Conaire under the hands of his foes. He will die—he will die."

" Let the earth crack, but I have sworn as my

tribe swears," said Fer Rogain. "Ingcel has chosen the Hostel of Da Derga."

"I choose it," said Ingcel, and his voice carried over all the hollow.

"It is yours." Fer Rogain's voice carried as far.

Fer Gair and Fer Le, the brothers of Fer Rogain, put their heads on their wrists across their knees and groaned deeply, and a moaning sigh swept the circles where the reivers of Erin crouched on the slope. But no man except Lomna Druth raised his voice against the decision that Fer Rogain had made. His oath bound them all. Lomna Druth, that mad prophet, was not to be silenced.

"Woe—woe—woe!" he threatened them in a shriek. "Woe to ye who wreak! Ye will die. I see the death-cloths in the air over ye. Do not let Ingcel one-eye fool ye! Take heed! Know ye the heroes who hold the hostel? Conaire, Conall Cernach, MacEcht, Cormac Condlongas, Cuscrad Menn, Clotach the Red. Six men for the six open doors! Were no other men in the hostel these six would hold the doors against ye till help came to them from the Wave of Cliona and the Wave of Assaroe. Are you not afraid, Ingcel one-eye?

"Fear is on you as a cloud, worthless warrior, shedder of kingly blood. You are afraid to die.

"Die—die—die! Woe is me before ye all! Woe is me after ye all! I see my body headless walking three steps. I see my head falling between wide door-posts, thrown out and in amongst chariot wheels. I see you, Flann one-hand." He whirled at Flann, froth on his lips. "I see you, your back to the wall and my knife at your throat. I will make you my fifth before I go——"

Fer Rogain caught him fiercely at the shoulder and hurled him to the ground, and he lay twitching at his brother's feet.

"It is finished." Ingcel raised his voice. "Let the men march by where I stand, each dropping his stone at my feet."

And under their leaders the men filed by, Gael and Briton and Pict, and each, after the ancient custom, dropped a stone at Ingcel's feet. There were eight stones short of eight hundred in that cairn that was built—a cairn of death if the destruction failed. But in victory each man would take up his stone, and what were left would be a cairn of remembrance. It is said that two hundred stones were left in that cairn and that it still exists somewhere in the Glen of the Bruden south of Dublin.

Two men, only, dropped no stone.

Flann was one of the two. He stood for a while at Ingcel's shoulder, saying nothing, and then he spaced his words between the clack of the falling stones.

"My work is done. If you are finished with me I will go."

After what seemed a long time Ingcel answered him, not turning his head.

"There is death in this, Flann one-hand."

"Here—now? That will be best."

"No—no! The struggle to-night was between us two, and I won. It is in me to be sorry that I won. Why should I kill?"

"I am a fool," said Flann. "I must go now."

"Must you go?"

Flann kept his voice low.

"There was a woman."

"I know. Our minds run together, Flann, you will remember. It is that one woman that is in my mind when I told you there was death in this. But if you must go, go quickly! I do not see the end."

And Flann's feet took him down the glen in spite of himself and his bitter mockery.

The second man that did not drop a stone was mad Lomna Druth.

His body stopped twitching, and he looked sideways under his chin at Ingcel's back. Then he crawled close to the dying fire, and drew from the ashes a dead pine branch glowing redly at the end. He blew softly at the glow, and a wisp of flame lifted after his breath. He cupped the flame with his hand, came to his knees, to his feet, his eyes fleering about him. No one was heeding him. He took two wary steps, and came suddenly to mad life.

He burst between two men, and, yelling high and shrill, went up the hill in the leaps of a wildcat, the now flaming branch above his head. His brothers, Fer Gair and Fer Le, pursued him, and grappled with him high on the breast of the hill, but already he had thrust his branch into a bank of furze, and the furze was high blazing. It was his final effort to save Conaire with a warning beacon.

The banners of flame writhed into the sky and lit up all the valley. They shone on Flann going down by the stream, and Flann lifted up his heels and ran.

## CHAPTER XXI.

### The Wetting of Sword Edges.

EVERYTHING was still in the Bruden of Da Derga, and everything watchful. Every man was awake, and the one woman was awake, too. Instead of the weight of sleep on the house there was a drawn-out tenseness pulling at the mind. The hounds in the kennels had not yet started barking. The windows no longer showed light, but a new-lit bonfire burned on the cooking platform above the river, and the glow of it shone dimly, redly down the seven long wide passages to the outer doorways. That was the only light, but it was enough for men to kill by.

Conaire the King was a man of peace, but MacEcht, Conall Cernach, and Cormac Condlongas were men of war. Trained in many a hard campaign at home and overseas they knew all the arts of foray and defence. The ominous portents of many days heavy on their minds, they took a hill-top blazing suddenly at night at its own meaning, armed every man who could bear arms—and every man could—and set all the skill and cunning of their trade to make the hostel a fort and an engine barbed with death Their method was simple and bold, yet marvellously cunning.

They barricaded no doorway. They even unhinged the one door that was shut in the eye of the wind. The seven doorways, like the doorways of the time, were wide enough to take two men abreast, but, from stone tread to lintel, not more than five feet high. The only barrier they set against a sudden drive was a strong bronze chariot chain hooked and rehooked between the jambs, thigh high. That was simple yet effective, inviting yet deadly, for an attacker must crawl under it or dive head first over it.

Three long paces back from the doorway, in the middle of the passage, for everyone to see, stood the door-ward, his long, oblong shield covering him from knee to eye, a throwing spear ready in his hand and a brace ready against the wall. At each side of the outer doorway, out of sight from without, two men were stationed armed with sword or mace or axe. In each of the seven doorways down the length of the passage two men were waiting in the dark. Any attack strong enough, desperate enough, with enough men still on their feet to force door and passage and win to the central courtyard, must there face the final reserve of picked men who guarded Conaire and his prince.

That was the plan : simple, bold, and deadly :
inviting attack and ready to break it most terribly.
That was why the drawn wire of tenseness strained
in that house so seeming quiet, so full of deadliness.

Conaire the King, without arms or harness, only
half believing that an attack was possible in this his
peaceful realm, went through the red-lit passages
one by one, looked in at each dark doorway, said a
quiet word to the watchers, went on again.

At the fifth outer doorway he found four men
and a woman, and the woman had a leather targe
below left elbow and a long, shining iron sword in
her hand. Cormac Condlongas, that cunning man,
had stationed them there, saying : " If ye fight ye
fight, and if ye do not ye will be the first of the
kill—from behind." And behind he had set eight
of his own Ulster bodyguard. And Clotach the
Red, looking at him underlidded, had said mildly :
" Remembering all the Ulster men I have killed I
will remember that for you in another place, son of
Conchobar the Wanton."

The King looked them over, where they leant
against the wall at each side of the doorway, and
shook his head sadly.

" All my poor geasas that I did not heed ! "

" Your geasas, but your men, too, O King,"
said Clotach.

" Yet you fared stubbornly before me in red and
mocked me with a song."

"With a song warned you from the hostel."

"Then you knew the danger?" the King put quickly.

"I knew, lord, but was bound to silence. The best I could do was to try and turn you with your geasa."

"You did your best," agreed the King quietly, and looked at Flann. "Were you, too, bound to silence, man-with-one-hand, that strangely urged me to feast on your black swine?"

"I was not bound, lord, but I was silent."

"Will you be silent now?"

Flann did not hesitate for a moment.

"There are eight hundred reivers coming down the glen of the Dothra, close at hand, to sack this hostel."

"Eight hundred! They must be from overseas. Who leads them?"

"Ingcel one-eye of Cumbria."

"Ingcel the Terrible, who taught Cuchulain!" He smiled sadly shaking his head. "It is only just. I sent my foster-brother, Fer Rogain, to reive him."

"They met—on the sea south of Falga."

The King started. "And Ingcel destroyed them?"

"No, lord. They parleyed and made a pact, oath for oath. A raid on Erin for a raid on Britain."

The King considered that and then said slowly :

" Fer Rogain and his four hundred are here with Ingcel ? "

" They are here, lord."

" Does he know that I am here ? "

" He knows."

" You do not know Fer Rogain." The King was near to smiling. " I know him. He will not turn his sword against me. I know him."

" Wait, lord ! " said Flann. " The raid on Britain came first. I was there. Ormlyth was burned to the ground, Gabur, its prince, and three hundred men slain ; and, lord, in the house of Ormlyth that night was Ingcel's father, Cormac the King of Britain, and with him his seven sons."

" They died ? "

" Under the swords of Fer Rogain and his brothers."

" They died," repeated the King softly, and looked at the ground.

" They died, and Ingcel chose this house in his turn."

" And in turn I am in this house to-night. It is just."

" You will not die while life is in us," said Clotach fiercely, " and then you will not die."

The King, eyes on ground, did not heed him.

" It is so—it is so," he whispered. " I know him, Fer Rogain, my brother. Let it be so."

He lifted his head and shook his own troubles off his shoulders. His blue clear eyes were on the woman.

"Better for you, dark one, though you carry a long sword, to hide in the furze till this is over."

"She will not, the foolish one!" Flann spoke quickly. "But you are the King and can command her."

Dairne looked bold-eyed at the King.

"The King can command me, and I will go out into the hands of his foes."

"That is how she talks," said Flann angrily.

"Women are like that, I am told," said the King, and, turning on his heel went slowly down the passage, hands behind him.

"That man will never die," said Clotach.

"He will die," Flann told him bitterly, "and we will die—" he turned to Dairne at his side— "and you will die, too, foolish one."

"Death is kind, Flann, but I do not feel it near me," she told him. And savagely he answered her.

"The thing that takes death's place will not be kind."

"Then make sure that I die."

Clotach, at Flann's other side, close to the jamb of the door, touched him with his elbow.

"Flann, brother, this is not your fight. Take the woman and go!"

"That is good advice," Flann agreed.

"Go, then, while there is time."

"I will go if you go," offered Dairne.

"Always I know good advice when I hear it," said Flann, mocking himself. "Once, my great brother Delgaun, gave me the wine of advice and, 'Good man yourself, Delgaun,' said I. But next morning I went away carrying a foolish long sword, and came back with a red stump at the end of my right arm. I am afraid. I feel my heart hollow. You, myself, my desire urge me to go, but I will stay here a little longer. That is the fool I am."

"You are the sort of fool that I like," said Clotach.

"H-u-s-h!" hissed Dairne. "They are near. My nose smells them." And she pressed her shoulder against Flann's, and turned wide, deep-set brown eyes on him.

"Even so. I will stay a little longer."

"Wait ye!" whispered Conal, the man of hearing, and set an ear on the edge of the other jamb. "Indeed and indeed! Feet—feet—feet swishing in heather, brushing in furze—a stone turning—harness creaking—a shield touching a sword edge. They are many." He straightened up and looked across at Flann. "Both sides of the house, brother! You are late."

"I would go now if I had a chance," said Flann, and grinned sardonically.

"My spear is ready for them and for ye," warned the Ulster guard, three paces down the passage.

"You will die to-night or to-morrow, Ulster man," Clotach warned him in turn.

And on his last word the hounds in the kennels began to bay. All night long they bayed. In the lulls of the tumult their raving and their howling made the mad night madder.

Yet, though the hostel was surrounded the attack was long in coming. Ingcel and Tulchinne were as able men of war as any man inside the hostel, and would have a plan of their own. Already, in the evening, Ingcel had looked over the position, and knew the lie of land and water. He would use that knowledge now. No doubt, men were crouching ready round the full circle of the hostel, looking, through the chariot wheels and between the door-wards' legs, down the long red-lit quiet pasages to where the fire glowed in the court-yard. They would know that a trap was set and would wonder where the spring lay. But at base the thing was simple. The hostel must be taken, and taken in Ingcel's way. He could set it ablaze with some loss of men, but, since the raid was for spoil, he would not resort to fire unless all else failed. A direct attack must come early or late, and both sides knew that.

When the attack came it came surprisingly, and

it came first at that fifth doorway. There was no challenge, no slogan, no rush of feet on the cobbled pavement, no sound at all above the baying of the hounds, but suddenly there was a head under the bronze chain across the opening. A head with tossing lint hair and yellow pale eyes wide-blazing! Like a fox, like a weasel, like an otter in the water, with one swift, lithe twist of body, Lomna Druth was inside the door and upright on his feet. While a man might draw a long breath, surprise, or that strange slowness to strike first, held them still. But mad Lomna was not still. Teeth bare, eyes concentrated to a point, he poised his black-hafted iron knife.

" My fifth, one-hand! " and he launched himself like a wolf at Flann.

Flann had no shield on his maimed right hand, but he had put aside his iron-forked staff for a thrusting spear. He hurled himself away from the wall and tried to bring his point to attack, but Lomna Druth struck it aside with his open hand, and, crouching, drew back his knife for the deadly upward groin rip. And as he crouched, Dairne's blade took him cleanly. Her long white arm made the terrible full circle, and her long keen blade hissed and sheared.

Lomna Druth's body jerked upright, whirled round, walked three paces, and crashed between the door-ward's legs, and the door-ward wasted a spear. Lomna Druth's head fell on Clotach's toes.

Clotach yelled and leaped. He placed a foot under the head in which the open eyes were blinking and hurled it out into the dark. They heard it strike the chariot wheel. There was a brief pause, and then the head came hurtling back over the chain. Clotach was facing the doorway, his shield shoulder high and his sword ready. The head struck him below the breast bone. He gave a coughing grunt, doubled from the hips, and fell forward, his breast across the chain.

Flann saw the lifting flash of the sword outside, and, of sheer instinct, thrust his bronze hook forward at a slant above Clotach's neck. The falling blade crashed sideways off the bronze, and hook and blade rang on Clotach's red helmet. Flann felt the jar to his shoulder, but his left hand was free, and with all his might he drove his spear at the full lunge. He felt the check and yield, and a voice roared. Flann recovered his blade, and in the same motion bronze-hooked Clotach's collar and pulled him backwards. Both of them fell together, and Cetach set his feet astride of them.

And then the doorway was a press of fighting men, and the bronze chain strained and groaned. Cetach and Conal were busy, and the chain held. There was a crashing tumult round the full circle of the house, and the war-horns bellowed through the night.

Dairne stood against the wall, her blade ready, watching Flann, and Flann pulled Clotach to his feet. Clotach was getting his wind back, and as soon as he could gasp made use of his stentorian throat.

"Shields up, brothers! Shields up, and strike above the knee!"

That is what Conal and Cetach were doing. No man got inside the chain, and the Ulster guard had not to use his spear.

Three times Fer Rogain drove home the attack with all his might on the seven doors, and three times he failed. The die being cast, Fer Rogain's men were in a desperate mood to kill and die, but though they killed and died the hostel held. Once and again a door chain broke and men were fighting and slaying down the length of the passage, but no single attacker won to the courtyard.

After the third drive Fer Rogain drew off his men, and but for the baying of the hounds and an occasional bellow of a horn, there was quiet for a time. MacEcht and Conall Cernach took the opportunity to change the guards and get the dead and wounded into the courtyard. Nine men were dead. Cetach had a spear thrust in his shoulder, but was still strong on his feet.

Clotach as he went out into the courtyard was rubbing his breast bone, and Conal laughed at him.

"Now I know why you took Flann's part

against me," he said. "You knew fine he was going to save the bull neck of you."

"Who saved the bull neck of me? All I remember is a dunt in the belly and a dunt on my pot helmet. Who saved my neck?"

"Flann did, and it the quickest thing I ever saw."

Clotach had to hear, and hearing he threw one arm round Flann and the other round Dairne.

"The best blow struck to-night was the first one," he told her.

"It was," agreed Conal, "and it was the clout she hit me over in the corner there."

"The next time I take your part, Flann brother," said Clotach, "Conal will wonder what happened him."

"I am taking good care next time," said Conal, and grew boastful. "Did ye see how I held the door alone when Cetach, the fool, dropped his shield? I did that. Ingcel has his match in front of him this time. We can hold the door for seven days and seven nights, and help will be here from Tara. Life! but I need a drink."

"I will now drink the Dothra dry," said Cetach, the wounded one.

At that instant a fighting man gave a cry of dismay and pointed down at the bed of the river. All rushed to the stone steps fearing an attack by water from under the house walls, though a grill guarded the channel. There was no attack. There was worse. Where the water had run smoothly over clean pebbles there was now no water. There was only gravel wet-shining in the flare of the bonfire.

Cetach leaped down, scooped at the gravel, scooped again, but no water gathered in the hollow. He thrust a pebble in his mouth, sucked it, spat it out, tried another. Wet pebbles were no assuagement for men after fight and wounds, but wet pebbles were all they had—except the strong ale and spirits to add to their thirst.

Ingcel, indeed, was an able man of war. While Fer Rogain was attacking the doors, Ingcel had set the Picts and Britons to damming the river, breaking down the banks of the stream and turning it into an old channel, the channel it had flowed in before Da Derga had turned it under his house.

The plight of the hostel was now a bad one. Conaire knew it. Conall Cernach and Cormac Condlongas knew it. Even MacEcht, desperate soldier, had to admit it.

" I have done without water for three days," said Conall Cernach, " but even you, MacEcht, could beat me the third day."

" My tongue black after a seven-day thirst," MacEcht told him sourly.

" Peace, children ! " Conaire quieted them.

"Three days! We can expect no help in three days."

"Then we are past help," said Conall Cernach, clear and cold as ice. "Nothing is left us but the sallying."

"Sallying let it be," growled MacEcht.

This practice of sallying was a peculiarly Gaelic and deadly method of warfare. The last desperate effort in defence, a forlorn hope to break the spirit of the attack, the forerunner of death, the refusal of stark men to accept defeat and parley. It was a drive of men to kill and kill again, and the method of it was simple and formalised. Two heroes—never more than four—made a sudden drive from a certain doorway and tried to make the circuit of the place beleaguered, killing as they went. If successful they came in by the same doorway. That was all. Not many made a full circuit, but many died.

The sallying that mad night lasted four hours—until the dawn. Some of the menials made the sally to escape, and one or two did break through, but as long as the King lived no fighting man would do that.

Conall Cernach and MacEcht, knowing each other for the best man in the hostel, made the first sally, going opposite ways. They made the full circuit and came in together by the same door. Fer Le and another had died under MacEcht's battle axe, and MacEcht had two wounds. Conall Cernach had cut down three; the top of his red shield had been shorn away by Fer Rogain, and his shield arm wounded.

Cormac Condlongas and Cuscrad Menn of Ulster made the sally, but Cuscrad did not make the re-entry.

Then Conaire himself, who had gone without arms all night, put on his harness, sternly silencing all protests with stern hand and stern eye.

"I make this alone," he said. "It is the King's way."

He made the full circuit and his virgin sword was red. But red, too, was his white tunic above the right breast; and after a time he coughed behind his shield and shut his lips tight on a bright red stain.

The three red hounds of Cualla made the sally then. Clotach went one way, and Conal and wounded Cetach went the other. Clotach made the circuit and waited for his brothers in the doorway, his shield up against the thrown javelins of the Picts. Conal came racing up through the gloom shouting.

"Cetach is down. Mane Unslow got him and I got Mane——"

A thrown spear took him between the shoulder blades and he fell on Clotach's shield. Clotach

Dairne came and sat at his side, and laid her sword on the stone flags.

" I know the thing in your mind, man," she said close to his ear.

He did not heed her till she placed her hand on his arm, and then he looked aside at her between thumb and forefinger. She put a finger below her young breast

"There ! " she said. " When the end comes, there ! It will not be long now. There ! Let me look at you with clean eyes in the Land of Youth."

" Is it the only way, Dairne ? "

" It is the only way that I see now."

Flann moved his head heavily between his hands.

" The Land of Youth ! You that had no youth will be young then. I do not know—I do not know at all ! "

# CHAPTER XXII.

## *The King Dies.*

DAWN at last, and the grey dawn came in greyly over the high roof of the hostel. In the courtyard, where the platform came to the channel of the river, were Conaire and his little Le Fri Flait, Conall Cernach, MacEcht, Cormac Condlongas, Clotach of Cualla, Oswald of East Britain, Flann of the left hand, and Dairne the woman. There was also the small black swine. He was tied to a pillar of the platform, and to the weary baying of the hounds replied with a weary, warrior grunt. There was no other living thing within the walls of the hostel.

Conaire the King lay on folded cloaks, and he was dying. There was a red froth on his lips, and he was barely conscious. His little son, Le Fri Flait, sat at his side holding one hand, and the youth's eyes and the youth's mind were dazed.

The King moved his head wearily and whispered :

" My spirit will not pass but with water. Let me drink ! "

Conall Cernach looked down into the bed of the stream, and then threw his head up to the clear thin sky of the morning where no cloud promised. Blood trickled down his sword arm. His red shield was only a fragment, and his shield arm was slashed to the bone. His voice was thick and hoarse.

"The King asks a drink of warriors. Where are the spencers that were menials to the King?" He glared at Dairne. "Woman of ill-omen, is there gall in your breasts for the King's mouth?"

MacEcht struck him open-handed and softly across the face, but Conall Cernach only laughed hoarsely.

"Now or in a little while, MacEcht! It does not matter."

MacEcht licked his blackened lips.

"The menials are dead," he croaked slowly. "They died like men. I will be the King's menial."

He clanked his broken shield on the ground, and his axe and helmet on top. His black tunic was caked with blood on his right side, and blood ran on his naked thighs. He bent to smooth Le Fri Flait's hair.

"Little one, we will try to keep the King's breed alive in Erin. Come!"

The prince, crying piteously, strained at the King's lax hand, but MacEcht loosed his fingers, picked him up under his right oxter, and went into the house. He went to the King's room, took the King's gold cup, and, without pause, strode down the long passage and out at the front door. There he stopped and looked around him. He did not see the valley opening to the immense dim plain of Ath Cliath, the brown hills hazed with the gold of furze, the far brown summits already lit with the sun risen from the sea. All he saw was the wide curve of reivers, a spear-throw from the walls, acrouch like wolves waiting. He held his gold cup high and walked slowly forward, and Le Fri Flait clutched at his wounded side.

A tall man in a winged helmet came forward to meet him, sheathing his sword as he came. A black-browed iron man with one eye.

"You are Ingcel and a King," said MacEcht hoarsely. "A King dies and asks for water to let his spirit pass. Give me the fill of this cup, and, thereafter, I will come out unarmed to your sword."

Ingcel said only : "Come with me."

He took him through the ring of reivers and up by the channel of the river amongst the furze to where the water was dammed and turned aside. The water lipped the dam and at any moment might burst a little runlet over it.

MacEcht set Le Fri Flait on his feet, dipped his cup and gave the child to drink, and the child drank greedily. MacEcht looked up at Ingcel.

"Ingcel does not kill children?"

"Ingcel will not kill this one."

That is the last that is known for certain of Le Fri Flait. It is said that he died of grief and exhaustion there by the water. It is said that he wandered in the woods and died of a wolf's fang. It is said that Ingcel took him to Alba, and that he was the son that reigned there after Ingcel. He is not mentioned again by name.

MacEcht dipped the cup a second time and looked into the shimmering, enticing bottom of it.

"Drink, warrior!" Ingcel invited him.

But MacEcht shook his head and said :

"I thirst while Conall Cernach thirsts." And he strode back towards the hostel carefully holding his full cup. Ingcel came behind and spoke.

"Come with sword and shield."

"It is a King's word," said MacEcht, not turning his head. "When I give you your death-wound I will hold water to your mouth if I am able."

He went into the hostel, and Ingcel turned to his men, raising up his voice.

"Let no man enter till I give the word."

MacEcht brought his cup to the King, lifted up his head in the crook of his arm, and set the water to his lips  The King drank a little and moved the cup away with his hand.

"Drink ye in turn," he whispered.

MacEcht took one mouthful, spat it out, and handed the cup to Conall Cernach, who took one mouthful and spat it out. In turn the six men took one mouthful and spat it out, and the last mouthful was left for Dairne.

But Dairne did not put her mouth to it. She held the cup high, poured the water on the ground, and threw the cup from her. Her voice rang clear.

"So let his spirit pass."

MacEcht wiped the King's lips with the ball of his thumb and the King whispered:

"My man, MacEcht! In my heart I loved you before all the wise ones."

The King turned his head inwards on his soldier's arm, and the spirit went out of him in one breath.

MacEcht laid the head gently down, turned a corner of the cloak over the dead face, and rose to his feet.

"That is the end for my King," he said. "I will make my end now."

He picked up axe and shield, kicked his pot helmet into the river bed, and looked at Conall Cernach, a grim question in his eye, but no question on his lips.

"I am your man, brother, this time," Conall Cernach answered the look. "I will go at your right hand. Let the others follow if they will."

Clotach pulled himself up against the stiffening of his wounds.

"Ye are of Ulster and Britain," he said, "even you, MacEcht, are out of Connacht, but I am of the King's Tara. I will watch here by the body of the King. It is my due."

"I would stay with you, red man," said MacEcht, "but Ingcel has my word. Come on, Conall, son of Amorgen!"

Cormac Condlongas and Oswald went out behind MacEcht and Conall, but Flann and Dairne stayed behind with Clotach standing over his dead King.

There was the firm pad of marching feet down the passage as the four men went out to their last fight; then silence; then the crash of arms and the peal of voices; and after that silence.

## CHAPTER XXIII.

### *The Mercy of Ingcel.*

CLOTACH took command as was his soldier's right.

"It will not be long now," he said, looking at Flann with haggard, blood-shot eyes. "I am sorry, Flann, that there is no grief in me for you and Dairne. Death is an easy thing at the end. Stand here with me, your back to the wall, and Dairne will stand between us."

Flann did as he was bid, but he said no word. For hours he had spoken no word, whatever his thoughts. There was no reason in anything. He was only a piece in some mad game he did not understand. His own hunger had driven him from home, and Ingcel had taken his coming for an omen; and that omen had brought him, Flann, to this end—and he had lost his old hunger on the road, and found a new one that would not be sated. Did a good king die because he had broken foolish geasas? Or was he of no more use in the mad game? Would Dairne die now that she had taken her life in her hands to mould it? . . . But why think about it? All things were gone by like the water of the river. Let him put all things, all thoughts aside, and die dumbly like a dumb fool.

Dairne did not take her stand between them. She stood on the top of the terrace, looking down into the dry, faintly-smelling bed of the river, and as she looked her eyes widened. Her long arm pointed.

"Look! Water flowing!"

A small trickle was running close to the stone steps. It was enough. At once they knew the thirst that was in them. At least, there was still thirst in Flann. The two men sprang down, scooped a little pit in the gravel, lay flat on their stomachs, and, ear to ear, dipped their mouths deep in. They drank and drank and drank. Dairne was more dainty. She scooped a basin of her own, waited till the water cleared, drank three fills of her cupped hands, and laved her face and neck. Then she came up on the platform, and a wet black tendril of hair twisted on her white brow.

"There is a blow in me now," said Clotach back in position. "Why are they so long in coming for it?"

"The fear of the night is on them yet," Dairne said. "Ye put fear on them like chains. Any time since the heart of night they could have taken the house, but they were afraid death would strike them from empty doors.    They will come creeping.''

"But come they will and death with them.''

"It is strange, but I do not feel death near.''

She looked at Flann, thought deep in her lovely brown eyes, but Flann looked out over her head, and his smoky blue eyes were again full of weariness and again unafraid.

"I will not be long,'' said Dairne, and turning, she went into the house.

Flann gathered his silence close about him.

\*      \*      \*      \*      \*

Four men came out into the courtyard, striding slowly, striding steadily, their shields up and their swords ready.    They were Ingcel one-eye, Eiccel his brother, Tulchinne the Pict, and Fer Rogain, the last son of Donn Desa.    Four abreast, they halted at the mid platform and looked about them. There were many men in the courtyard, but, except two, they were all dead men.    The two stood against the wall above the water that trickled more strongly, and a tall woman stood between them.

As they looked the woman moved the two men apart with her hands, stepped down from the platform, and walked smoothly across the yard towards them.    They waited, and Tulchinne the Pict's red tongue licked between black beard.

She was a tall woman, and red-strapped sandals

285

peeped, striding straight-footed, below a long kirtle of green that clung to a young body of fire and light and honey. There was a red girdle low on her hips; and, whiter than ivory, her neck rose from a red selvedge low on her breast. Over each breast was a clasp of gold, and a gold-and-bronze brooch was set below her throat. Open sleeves fringed with silver showed the curve of her long white arms. Her left arm was banded with gold at the wrist, and her right above the elbow; and in her right hand she carried a dagger with a bronze leaf for blade. There was a broad band of silver holding her black hair, and a green stone burned in the middle of it on her white forehead above black brows. But the fire of that stone paled in the lustre of her deep-set, wide-set, hooded, insolent eyes. Her mouth was a red warm gash in the pallor of her face.

Two spear-lengths away she stood still, her head proudly up, and her eyes, insolent and beautiful, on Ingcel.

"You are Ingcel the King?" Low and deep her voice.

"I am Ingcel."

She placed her left hand between the clasps on her breasts.

"Look at me!"

"I am looking."

She kept the hand between her breasts. "For

the lives of these two men, Flann one-hand and Clotach the red.''

But Tulchinne of the Rapine threw back his black bullet-head, and his red tongue showed between his white teeth.

''Ho-ho-ho! I will take you and their throats cut.''

Ingcel put his sword into his shield hand, and looked calmly at Tulchinne over his right shoulder. Calm was his voice, too.

''It is in my mind these many days that Tulchinne has a habit of mouthing before the King.''

''It is a bad habit I could never get rid of,'' said Tulchinne grinning.

''Let this help you,'' said the King, and struck Tulchinne back-handed across the mouth.

Tulchinne was a squat man set on the ground massive as a bull, but he fell as from a mace blow. He lay on his back for a space, rolled over, scrabbled on the stones, and rose staggering to his feet. He spat out two teeth and blinked dazedly at his lord.

''I am King of the Picts,'' said that man. ''I will not use my hand next time. Go and set a guard on these doors, and see that no fire is lit till all the spoils are outside! Go!''

Tulchinne had no word to say this time. He went.

"I have seen you fight, Clotach the Red. It is your trade. I want a man at my back when Tulchinne remembers his broken mouth. You will come with me."

"Where Flann goes I go," said Clotach sullenly. "He holds my life."

"Say that when this talk is done and with him you may go."

He turned to Flann and frowned. Flann was not looking at him, but at the stones before his feet, and his long, still face could not be read.

"I know you best of all, Flann of Baravais, yet I do not know what to do with you."

Dairne, at Flann's side, answered for him.

"Send him to his own place, O King! He is soft-hearted and comes to hurt on every strange road."

"You know him, too, Dairne?" The King's eyes brightened on her. "Dairne! it is the name of the one woman. I will not say to you what you must do. What will you do?"

"He bought me with a band of gold," said Dairne in her low voice.

"Was it a price, Flann?"

"Since I met her," said Flann without looking up, "she has gone her own road and taken me with her. I did not know that till now."

"Take him home to his Baravais, Dairne," said Ingcel strongly. "Take him home and let him build a house for you." He smiled wistfully. "It may be that he will be able to stand the sight of a woman suckling her son. I am finished now."

"I am thinking, O King," said Clotach half-ruefully, " that watching I will be till the Pictman opens his broken mouth."

Flann lifted his head and looked at Ingcel.

" It is hard to be a King, O Ingcel, but it is not evil. You are master of Fate, but I do not understand any of this."

" Do not try now. You are alive and on a new road. Follow it, even if the end be bitter. That is the law for men."

And Flann was alive. He had just found it out. It surprised him. He was alive, yet he was not changed in any way. For when he spoke the old satiric twist was in his speech. He said :

" I will take Dairne—or she will take me—but this demon that is a small black pig I will not take."

And Dairne said :

" He is my dowry. It is the custom."

" Custom ! to drag a squealing small demon across the world for my brother Maur to put in a song ? "

But Dairne went to the pillar and untied the small pig, and as she untied it it gave little soft pig grunts that would make one wonder how a pig could grunt so nicely. She came and put the rope in Flann's hand.

"Try him once!"

Flann looked at her and tried to think of something completely devastating. There was nothing handy. He had to do something. He walked smartly across the courtyard and waited for the strain and the squeal that would give him the spirit to kick the demon into the river again running strongly. But the little beast trotted at his very heels, and when Flann paused and looked down open-mouthed, it nuzzled him, grunting happily, at the back of his knee.

Flann found himself smiling. He found his hand rubbing behind a flicking ear. He said:

"You know, he is a nice little black swine after all."

"Flann soft-heart," said Dairne softly.

# CHAPTER XXIV.

## *The Last Word.*

IT was a high-summer dawn, with gossamer pearl on the grass, that Dairne waked at Flann's side under the brown cloak. She turned over on her face and propped herself on her elbows. She was looking up a wide rocky valley with a slowly lifting floor between the flanks of mountains, and the mountains were tall and serrated and carried snow in their northern folds. Up that rocky valley, over the pass, and down the southern slow slope was Long Baravais, a day's march away.

Dairne's shoulders stirred and her nose twitched. She was shy. She was frightened. Before set of sun she would be facing Flann's father, Orugh, and Flann's brothers, Delgaun and Maur, and, worse than all, she would have to face the scrutiny of Alor, the red-haired wife of Delgaun. She did not want to think about that meeting, but the thought came.

She drew her side close to Flann's, put an arm over him and rested her shoulder on his breast.

She examined his sleeping face carefully. Calm as the sky it was, and serene ; and his gentle, firm mouth had no quirk. There was just one small line from nostril to mouth-corner, and she tried to smooth it out with a gentle finger tip.

" You will be mindful of me, my heart," she whispered.

Flann's lip twitched. He stirred and opened his eyes. First he smiled and then he grumbled.

" This an hour to wake a man ? "

" Flann sleepy-head ! "

" I did not sleep a wink."

" You did. There is a fear in me, Flann."

" That is no bad thing, but rare in a woman."

" To-night—there is your father, Orugh ! What will he say to me ? "

" He will bite your nose off—and you with no nose to spare."

" Your brothers—no ! They will like me, I think."

" Wait till you hear Delgaun's growl and Maur's song."

" Delgaun will give me his son to hold, and I will help Maur with his song. There are two verses in my mind already."

" Let me up, and I will make back for Cumbria."

" I am holding you. It is Alor that I fear, Alor that you loved—that loved you—a little ! How will she look at me ? "

"Down her nose, and it is no short one."

"I have a look, too. Will they let us build our house near them?"

"They will not," said Flann firmly.

Her eyes widened in dismay. "Then we must go away. Oh, Flann!"

"Foolish one!" His good arm came about her. "Our house will be close at the left side of my father's house. Orugh and Delgaun and Maur, and myself sometimes, will build it in a week—with a stone chimney—and we disputing all the time. Alor will help a little with advice, and she turning eyes towards her own house afraid our house will be better."

"I will help with my hands. I am strong."

"You will be holding Delgaun's brat under your oxter and hindering us with changes."

"It will be a fine house and high in the roof-tree," she said proudly.

"It will be a fine house," Flann agreed. "I see it in my mind's eye. I dreamt it. I saw it. I heard you crooning in it."

"What did I croon?" she asked softly.

"It was a very foolish croon," Flann told her. She drew her breast on his.

"Tell me, Flann! Tell me your dream."

"I will not tell you my dream."

"Then I think I will go to sleep for a little while."

"You will not. You will get up and gather sticks for my morning meal."

"Here is the first of it for you," whispered Dairne, and set her mouth down on his. His arm tightened.

The small black pig, nosing in unprofitable ground, grunted disgustedly and went farther afield in search of his own breakfast. Let the small black pig have the last word. If his grunt said anything it said :

"The poor foolish young ones ! "